PRAISE FOR T

C000104266

"Daring, sophisticated, and literary.... Exactly what good erotica should be." — **Kitty Thomas on *The Siren***

"Kinky, well-written, hot as hell." — **Little Red Reading Hood on *The Red: An Erotic Fantasy***

"Impossible to stop reading." — **Heroes & Heartbreakers on *The Bourbon Thief***

"Stunning.... Transcends genres and will leave readers absolutely breathless." — ***RT Book Reviews* on the Original Sinners series**

"I worship at the altar of Tiffany Reisz!" — ***New York Times* bestselling author Lorelei James**

A WINTER SYMPHONY

A Winter Symphony: A Christmas Novella

Copyright © 2020 Tiffany Reisz

All rights reserved. No part of this publications may be reproduced, stored in a retrieval system, or transmitted, in any form or by any means, electronic, mechanical, photocopying, recording, or otherwise, without the prior written permission of the publisher, 8th Circle Press, Louisville, Kentucky, U.S.A.

All characters appearing in this work are fictitious. Any resemblance to real persons, living, or dead, is purely coincidental.

An un-edited draft of "A Beautiful Thing" previously appeared on TiffanyReisz.com.

Trade Paperback ISBN: 978-1-949769-18-0

Cover design and title page by Andrew Shaffer. Includes elements licensed from Shutterstock.com.

www.8thcirclepress.com

First Edition

TIFFANY REISZ

A Winter Symphony

8TH CIRCLE PRESS
LOUISVILLE, KY

CONTENTS

A WINTER SYMPHONY

AUTHOR'S NOTE

Readers who have read the Original Sinners series through *The Mistress* (book 4) can read *A Winter Symphony* without fear of spoilers.*

Between *The Mistress* and book 5, *The Saint*, the Unholy Trinity decamp from New York to New Orleans. Here is the story of how and why that move came about...and no, it was not because of the beignets. Although that was a factor.

❄

**Readers new to the Original Sinners series should start with the first book,* The Siren. *A complete reading order can be found at TiffanyReisz.com.*

DEDICATED TO BETHANY HENSEL,
MERCI, MON AMI

FIRST MOVEMENT

NOVEMBER ALLEGRO

ALLEGRO:

At a brisk, lively, or cheerful tempo.

CHAPTER ONE

KINGSLEY WAS HAPPY.

Very, very happy.

This came as a surprise to him. It would have come as a surprise to anyone who knew him, too.

On the list of adjectives frequently used to describe him, one might find the following:

- dangerous (of course)
- sexy (he had his fans)
- sleazy (he also had his detractors)
- ruthless (fact)
- insane (not quite, though he had his moments)
- brooding (fair point—he was French, after all, and contemplating the ultimate meaninglessness of his own existence was in his DNA)

But one would not include "happy" on any list describing Kingsley.

Apparently, he needed a new list, because now he was a very happy man. True happiness, that is—*joie de vivre*, joy in living.

Had he ever felt this depth of joy before? Maybe once? Maybe on the last warm autumn night in Maine, when he was sixteen and Søren seventeen? Maybe that moment, after the beating and after the sex, when he lay across Søren's lap under the wild stars? Maybe that moment when Søren's fingers stroked Kingsley's naked back, tender from welts, and softly said three words...

You did well.

Yes, that was the last time he'd felt this much happiness. Once, he might have thought it would be the only time he'd ever feel it, until the night Juliette said three even more beautiful words to him.

Je suis enceinte.

The reality of this newly-discovered *joie* occurred to him on the night of his forty-seventh birthday. November 2nd in a year when winter came early, rudely shoving autumn out of the spotlight. Outside it was cold enough to chip teeth from chattering. Inside Kingsley's small private sitting room in his Riverside Drive townhouse, it was warm, however. The fire burned cheerfully behind the grate. He'd forgone his usual after-dinner wine for a milky cup of coffee —decaf—and he held Juliette lightly against his chest as they lay on the large antique fainting sofa. Out of nowhere, Juliette gasped as if in pain. A gasp followed by a laugh. She grabbed

Kingsley's hand and put it on the swell of her pregnant belly.

"Someone is rehearsing for the Rockettes tonight," Juliette said, laughing again as she was kicked from within.

"Or there's a football practice going on in there," Kingsley said, feeling another tiny foot or hand press against his palm. The wave of joy rushed over him, leaving his head swimming and his throat almost too tight to speak.

"Back to sleep, Coco," Kingsley said softly to Juliette's stomach. "It's past your bedtime."

Coco wasn't the baby's name. They'd already decided on Céleste for a girl, Hugo for a boy (after author Victor Hugo). In French, *coco* was a child's slang term for an egg. At one of Juliette's early obstetrician appointments, her doctor had said their growing fetus was now about the size of an egg.

"I think Coco's trying to tell you 'happy birthday,'" Juliette said as she eased onto a pile of silk cushions. She wore a silk turquoise bathrobe, the tie of which kept sliding over her belly and under her breasts now that her narrow waist was long gone.

Kingsley put his mouth to her stomach. "Is a card in the mail too much to ask?"

Juliette smiled tiredly and adjusted the pillows underneath her as Kingsley drew her long and lovely dark legs across his lap.

"Did you ever think at this time last year, *this* is how we'd be spending your birthday?" she asked. "Alone together. No party. No wine, even.

Just the two of us sitting here, being boring and reading?"

They were being very boring. Kingsley was almost finished reading *The Immoralist* by André Gide. Juliette was reading a book on her iPad, and he occasionally saw her smile at something in it.

Yes, this was certainly a very different scene from last year's birthday, which he'd celebrated in high and mad style. His townhouse had been bursting at the seams with guests dressed for the French Revolution, inspired by Kingsley's heritage and the upcoming release of the film *Les Misérables*, though the theme had not been *Liberté, égalité, fraternité* but *Liberté, égalité, sodomie...*

"This is better," Kingsley said.

"Are you certain?" she asked. Fear flashed across her dark eyes. They were lovers and they were in love, and this had been the case for several years. But they weren't married. Kingsley didn't practice monogamy, or even really believe in it. As for Juliette, she suffered from a marriage phobia, though he couldn't blame her. A rich, powerful man had once practically owned her, using her mother as leverage to keep her in his home and his bed. Men all over the city—especially Brad Wolfe, that asshole—showered her with gifts and attention and declarations of devotion. She played with them and took their presents, of course, and enjoyed every minute of it.

But now she and Kingsley were having a child together, and this easy open love affair of theirs was changing. A welcome change, she admitted, but Kingsley knew she worried that it wasn't so welcome for him.

After a long pause, he answered, "You know I've wanted children for as long as I can remember."

"I have wanted to dance on the moon since I was a little girl, but if NASA came to our front door and told me it was time to go, I would be terrified."

"I'm happy," he said. "This is what I want."

"I know it's what you want. But is it *all* you want?"

A good and fair question from the woman who was having their child. A question that had to be answered, if not that night then soon. Very soon. Little Coco wasn't going to wait forever for him to decide.

"Are you asking about Søren?" Kingsley said. He ran his hands up and down her smooth bare calves. She took long baths these days, enjoying the buoyancy of the warm water, and Kingsley would shave her legs for her now that she had trouble reaching her ankles. "Do you want me to give him up?"

"No," she said. "That's the last thing I want. Someone has to beat you, and it's not going to be me. All I want to know is...is it enough for you? *Finally*, do you have enough?"

Kingsley started to answer, to say yes, of course it was finally enough, that she had nothing to fear, that nothing and no one was going to come between them.

There was a knocking at the front door—loud, insistent. Juliette sat up and put her hands protectively over her stomach.

Kingsley jumped to his feet. More pounding on the door. Shouting now. It sounded like someone was trying to beat their way into the house. Kingsley looked at Juliette. "Stay here," he said.

He left the sitting room and strode down the hall to the grand front doors, wishing he still had his dogs. As he neared the doors, he heard his name and drunken laughter. The tension eased. He unlocked the door.

A half dozen men and women stood on his front porch wearing *outré* party clothes under their coats.

"Long live the King!" one woman shouted, hefting a bottle of champagne in the air. "About time! I'm freezing my tits off."

She and the other intruders started to press toward the door. Kingsley held up his hand. "What the hell are you all doing here?"

"It's your birthday, right?" the woman with the champagne bottle said. "We're here for the party."

He recognized her. Her name was...something that started with an R? Manhattan socialite—she'd tried on kink like a new outfit and decided she liked the way it looked on her. He recognized a few other faces, men and women who'd frequented his clubs in the past. Kat, the daughter of the ex-governor. Tate, her high-functioning alcoholic boyfriend. Another girl wearing only a red, white, and blue bikini under her coat. In the old days, he might have saluted her flag. Tonight he just wanted to tell her to wrap up before she contracted hypothermia.

"*Mon roi?*" Against orders, Juliette had come out of the sitting room and now stood by him. "Who is it?"

"Oh," Roxy said, eying Juliette's round belly. Kingsley instinctively moved in front of Juliette. "No party this year, I guess?"

"No," Kingsley said to Roxy, to Kitty, to Tate, to the city itself. "The party's over."

CHAPTER TWO

AFTER THE REVELERS HAD LEFT, Juliette laughed at how scared they'd been of a few drunks at their door. She kissed him on the lips and went up to bed. Kingsley promised to be up soon. First, he had to check all the locks.

He wandered from room to room, not only checking that the front, back, and side doors were locked, but the windows, too. Never before had he locked the doors of the townhouse, believing it a sign of fear and weakness. His old arrogance shamed him. The woman he loved was pregnant with his first child.

He was almost tempted to hire bouncers to guard the door. After checking the locks, he returned to the sitting room to make certain the fire was out completely. How could he live with himself if he let the townhouse catch on fire with Juliette inside? Was this paranoia? He wished. But no, just weeks ago, secrets from his past had finally caught up with him. Søren and Nora had nearly paid with their lives. At night, as soon as he closed his eyes, he was back in that room, ears ringing from the loud claps of gunshots, and there was every chance in the world he would not survive to hold his newborn baby.

Everything changed in that room. And everyone came out of that room a different person from the one who'd walked into it. Especially him. The man who went in never locked his doors. The man who came out checked the seals on the windows to make sure not even an ant could crawl inside his home.

A mirror hung over the fireplace, gilt-framed, antique, and he caught a glimpse of the King that looked back at him—dark olive skin inherited from his Italian grandfather, dark eyes. Not a single gray hair, not a single wrinkle despite this being his forty-seventh birthday. Thanks to his good genes he didn't remotely look his age.

Ah, but he felt it. Here he was, creeping toward fifty and yet still kicking drunks off his stoop at midnight.

Roxy had looked at him like he'd grown a second head when he'd opened the door. It was his attire—no suit, no boots. Instead, he had on dark brown trousers, a black pullover, and the glasses he wore when reading. He looked, in a word, vanilla.

A year ago, he might have cared. Maybe even a few months ago. But the moment Juliette began to show, the moment when her pregnancy became real and not hypothetical, was the moment he stopped giving a single fuck about anyone and anything but her, the baby, and the few people in his life he considered family.

Nora. Søren. Griffin...

The list was short and getting shorter all the time. The dogs were gone. Sadie had been killed, and Dom died not long after. Old age. Brutus and Max were living with Calliope in the Hamptons. He'd lied to Juliette, saying since the dogs were so old, he wanted their last months to be spent somewhere they could run and play by the water, not cooped up in the townhouse. But the truth was, the first time he'd seen one of his enormous Rottweilers jump up on Juliette, nearly knocking her over, he couldn't get them out of the house fast enough.

God, he needed a drink. Except since Juliette wasn't drinking, he'd also cut back.

The dogs living with Calliope? Staying home on his birthday to snuggle up with Jules and read? No wine? He knew becoming a parent entailed making sacrifices. So far, they'd all been surprisingly easy. He couldn't help but wonder what harder, more painful sacrifices were to come?

He placed his glasses on top of his book on the side table. Juliette had left her iPad behind, and he picked it up to take to her upstairs. He tapped the power button, curious to see what she'd been reading. The screen came to life and displayed a photograph of one of the most beautiful houses he'd ever seen. A red-brick mansion with white columns and a grand portico. Elaborate, almost tropical landscaping. He read the caption: "One of many mansions on St. Charles Avenue, seen from a New Orleans streetcar."

It was a page from a travel guide to New Orleans. No surprise, as he was taking her there the day after Christmas for a two-week "babymoon," which was like a honeymoon. Supposedly. He had never heard of such a thing until Griffin had told him it was *de rigeur* now to take one's pregnant wife or girlfriend on a last big vacation before the first baby came along. Sounded painfully bourgeois to him, but when he mentioned it to Juliette, her eyes had widened. She'd said at once, "Could we go to New Orleans?"

As he flipped through the pages of the book on her iPad, he saw massive ancient trees dripping with Spanish moss, old mansions, brightly-painted houses, Christmas lights hanging in palm trees, and French words everywhere —*Mardi Gras* (Fat Tuesday), *banquette* (sidewalk), *Vieux Carré* (Old Square, the French Quarter), and *bien sûr—laissez les bons temps rouler* (let the good times roll).

He wished they were leaving right now.

As he started up the stairs, his phone began buzzing in his back pocket. He pulled it out and saw he had a text message from Leo, one of the bouncers at The 8th Circle.

Guy ODed outside on the sidewalk. Ambulance on the way. Orders?

One of ours? Kingsley replied. If the man were a member of the club, he would head over there right away.

Never seen him before.

Kingsley told Leo to keep watch over the man, to keep him warm until the authorities arrived. And he should try to keep everyone inside the club until the police and EMTs were gone.

These calls were coming more and more often—poor souls overdosing in the bathrooms of his clubs, in the alleys behind them. Opioids were almost always the culprit. It seemed like a lifetime ago he'd found Griffin Fiske passed out drunk on the floor of one of his clubs. A more innocent time. Booze and coke were child's play compared to the *au courant* drugs people were on these days.

Kingsley knew these calls would keep coming. And people would keep showing up at his door, expecting an invitation into the non-stop orgy that had been his life for so many years.

When he said the party was over, he'd meant it.

But how did you un-invite an entire city to a party they'd thought would never end?

SECOND MOVEMENT

DECEMBER ADAGIO

ADAGIO:

At a slow tempo.

CHAPTER THREE

When Søren called, Kingsley answered. Even when the call was nothing more than an invitation to dinner.

In the late afternoon of a bright mid-December day, Kingsley drove himself to Wakefield. He parked the black BMW he used for private trips in the church's parking lot. As he walked to the sanctuary, he gazed up at the church. Bathed in the watery light of a winter sun, it looked like a Currier & Ives calendar. Perfectly picturesque. Pure New England. Before going inside to find Søren, Kingsley glanced around, taking in the scene, committing it to memory.

Usually, Kingsley looked forward to his nights with Søren with a sense of anticipation bordering on feverishness. Not today. It wasn't going to be easy being with his lover and not telling him the momentous decision he'd made. Six weeks ago, he'd asked himself how he could un-invite the whole city from the party that had been his life. Now he knew the answer.

If the party won't leave, you leave the party.

He had no plans to tell anyone what he had decided—not Søren, not Juliette, not anyone—until after the holidays. He didn't want to ruin Christmas, not after all they'd been through this year. Kingsley walked on toward the church.

Two enormous wreaths of greenery tied with red bows hung on the great double doors of Sacred Heart Catholic Church. He went inside, where he heard voices coming from the sanctuary. Sounded like an argument. One male voice, unmistakably Søren's. A younger woman's voice—not Nora's.

Kingsley poked his head through the doors and saw Søren sitting at the bench of the church's grand piano with a young woman—Maxine, who used to play soccer with them on Sacred Heart's intramural church league team. She was college-aged now, with short dark hair and an athlete's compact build. For some reason, she was thrusting her left hand out at Søren and pointing at it.

"One hard whack," she was saying. "That's all I ask."

Catholics were getting stranger all the time.

"What's going on?" Kingsley asked as he came to stand by Maxine. She turned to face him, gasped at the sight of him, and threw herself into his arms.

"King!" she yelled in delight.

"Missed you, too," he said, returning the embrace with affection.

She pulled back, but left her hands on his shoulders and gently shook him. "You're having a baby!"

"Not exactly," Kingsley said. "I've outsourced that part to Juliette."

"I'm so happy for you." Maxine shook him again. She really was a very sturdy girl. Kingsley's brain bounced around his skull like a pinball until she let him go.

"I'm very happy for me, too," he said. "Or will be when the concussion subsides."

Søren was watching this whole show with an expression of barely concealed amusement. He shook his handsome blond head, turned back to his piano, and played a few notes.

Maxine grinned, showing all her teeth. "Could you do me a favor, King?"

"Sexual?"

"Not today," she said. "Can you please tell Father S to hit me as hard as he can with a Bible?"

"No, no, no," Søren said, punctuating the no's with three descending notes on his piano.

"Why do you want him to hit you with a Bible?" Kingsley asked. "Other than the obvious."

"I have a tumor," she said, wincing.

"A what?"

"Maxine is exaggerating," Søren said. "She has a small ganglion cyst in her hand that requires minor medical attention, not being slapped with a Bible. Especially not by me."

"Look at it." Maxine held up her left hand and pointed to a tiny bump on the back near her wrist. "Isn't it disgusting?"

"Grotesque." Kingsley could barely see it.

"Right? It's called a Bible bump," she said. "It's called that because the way you're supposed to get rid of it is by hitting it hard as you can with a Bible to make it pop. Nobody around here can whack harder than Father S—"

"This is very true," Kingsley said.

"But he won't do it. Says it's 'assault on a parishioner' or some bullshit like that. Sorry, Father S."

"Assault or not, if you want your cyst gone, call a doctor," Søren said. "Hitting it with a Bible is an old wives' tale."

"Sexist," Maxine said.

"I'll do it," Kingsley said.

"Good Lord." Søren sighed and returned his attention to the piano, playing a slow, melancholy tune.

"Father S, do you mind?" Maxine said. "We're trying to do a medical procedure here."

Søren swiftly stood up, closed the fallboard on his piano, and walked out of the sanctuary.

"Thank God," Maxine said, shaking her head. "Now, will you really whack me with a Bible?"

"It would be an honor and a pleasure."

Kingsley never turned down an opportunity to take a whip, paddle, or a New Revised Standard Version Bible (red leather, how apropos) to an attractive young woman.

He had Maxine duck behind a pew and grip the rounded top, giving him a clean target. With her head down, she recited the Latin *Pater noster* in hushed tones. Kingsley narrowed his eyes, readied the heavy leather Bible, and just as he had hefted the holy book over his head, he felt it plucked from his hand.

"What?" Kingsley turned. Søren stood there, the Bible tucked under his arm.

"Here," he said and held out a small scrap of paper. "Maxine, you have an appointment this week with Dr. Liz Rayden, an orthopedist. She's booked until March, but she said she'd see you this week."

Maxine looked up at him and rolled her eyes. She stood up, took the paper, and tucked it in her pocket.

"Fine. Fine. See if I ever ask you for help again," she said. She threw her arms around Kingsley for another hug and said into his ear, "You're going to make a great dad, you know."

It was the sort of bland nicety people said to expectant parents, but Maxine had said it with such sweet and easy faith in him, he felt a lump in his throat. "*Merci*."

"And when your kid's big enough, they can join the Sacred Heart Attacks!"

"I still despise that team name," Søren said.

"You were outvoted," Maxine said. "Get over it." She released Kingsley from her hug and pointed at Søren. "Merry Christmas, and thanks for nothing. Me and my tumor are out of here."

She started for the door, and Søren began to say, "It's not—"

"Don't," Kingsley said. "Just don't."

"I can't believe you were actually going to hit Maxine's cyst with a Bible. What if you'd broken her hand?"

"There were two positive outcomes either way," Kingsley said. "Either it would work, and goodbye cyst. Or...she'd learn once and for all to listen to you."

"Fair play," Søren said.

A few minutes later, Søren locked up the church, and they started off down the path that led them through the small snow-shrouded woods and to the rectory.

In the last rays of daylight, the trees shimmered like diamonds.

"Stop," Kingsley said. "I need a picture of this. For Juliette." He took out his phone and snapped a few pictures of the scene—the light on the white trees, the little rectory hidden behind snowy branches.

Søren was staring at him as he took his pictures, studying him.

"What?" Kingsley said in French. "It's pretty."

"Yes, it is. It's pretty every year. First time you've ever bothered to notice."

Kingsley heard a question in that statement, but he refused to answer it. "Everything's different this year."

"That it is." Søren seemed to accept that as a good enough answer. They carried on, ducking under a canopy of tree branches and deeper into the little dark forest, made silver with snow. The moment they were out of the sunlight, the temperature dropped, but Kingsley didn't hurry toward the house, though it looked as cozy and inviting as a cottage out of a children's storybook. He inhaled the icy air, so clean and pure and cold, listened to the sound of the crisp snow breaking and crunching under his boots, a sound like no other. He even slipped his bare hand out of the pocket of his wool coat to gather snow off a low-hanging limb and feel it turn to water in his palm. If Søren hadn't commented about Kingsley's sudden interest in photography, he would have tried taking a few more pictures—the dark trees, the snowy path, the cottage with the gray stone chimney patiently waiting for a fire.

And Søren... He wanted a hundred, a thousand, a million pictures of Søren. Especially the picture of him he was tattooing onto his memory, Søren just as he was right then and there—tall and blond (with a touch of silver, just like the trees), and starkly handsome in his black coat with his Roman collar peeking out of the open top button.

He wanted to record everything, every sight and sound, every taste and smell. Not for Juliette, as he'd said. For himself. A king and a priest walking through a snowy wood... It sounded like the beginning of a story. The beginning, not the end.

They entered the rectory through the kitchen door, and Søren shucked off his coat with one casual move, slipped his finger under his dog collar and popped it out of his shirt. Kingsley hung his own coat on the hook.

"Where did you want to go to dinner or—" he started to say but then was cut off by Søren pushing his back against the door and kissing him.

The kiss was hot as summer but tasted like winter—that pure electric taste of ice-cold air that made the blood wake and the skin shiver. The kiss was possessive, and Kingsley let it possess him. He surrendered his weight against the door and lifted his chin to give Søren more of his mouth. There they were, those hands on his neck, holding him in place. Those hands he'd spent years wanting, dreaming of, remembering like a man in prison remembers the best meal he ever had in his life...

Kingsley returned the kiss—with his mouth, with his tongue, with his hands seeking Søren's skin at his throat, his beautiful bare throat. Kingsley found that perfect hollow with his fingertips.

The kiss broke, leaving them standing at the door close together, breathing each other's breaths.

"No dinner," Søren said. "You. Upstairs."

"Here?"

Søren smiled. "Why not?"

"We've never...here."

"Yes, we have."

"With Nora. Not alone."

"Really? Never?"

"Never," Kingsley said.

"I thought for sure..."

"You must have imagined it."

"I did imagine it," Søren said. "More times than I'll admit to."

"Admit to it," Kingsley said. "Please."

Søren laughed softly, though Kingsley wasn't joking. They had gone to bed together at the rectory many, many times over the years, always with Nora there between them. Never alone, never just the two of them, not here. There were two things Kingsley wanted in his life, wanted so badly he would have sold everything he owned down to his very soul: to have Søren, and to have children with Juliette.

And now, as if by magic, the universe had handed him both at the same time. But it was a trick, he realized. He was given both. He could keep only one.

"How many times?" Kingsley asked again. "I want to know. I spent too many years thinking you didn't want me at all. No more secrets, no more lies. I'm asking—how many times did you want to call me and ask me over, but you told yourself no?"

"I didn't count," Søren said, still smiling as if Kingsley were joking. But then, as if he finally saw how serious Kingsley was, he said, "Not even I can count that high. Is that what you want to hear?"

"Yes."

"Good. Now are we going to stand here in the kitchen while you ask me questions all night, or are you going to come upstairs with me so I can beat and fuck you?"

And while Kingsley did want answers...

Reader, he went upstairs with him.

CHAPTER FOUR

TONIGHT WOULD BE the first time they played alone together in Søren's bedroom. And eventually, one night would be their last time. So when Kingsley followed Søren up the stairs of the rectory to his bedroom, he counted the steps—eleven. And he memorized the particular shade of sunlit gold that gilded the dark hardwood floors. And the smell... The rectory was tended by the world's most Italian Catholic grandmother, and it always smelled clean, like pine and fresh linens. And winter, of course. It always smelled like winter, even in summer, because the man who made this little cottage his home smelled like winter. His skin like snow. His hair like ice. And, once upon a time, Kingsley would have said his heart was frosted over like a windowpane on a January morning, but what man with a heart of ice could say something like, "Not even I can count that high," when asked how many times he'd imagined them making love in his bedroom?

Once inside that bedroom, Søren went to the window and drew the white curtains open. There was nothing like the last light on a winter's day, the way it filled a room with a strange and sacred silence.

Kingsley felt almost light-headed. He leaned against the bedpost to steady himself.

"I still can't get used to it," Kingsley said breathlessly when Søren turned to face him.

"What can't you get used to?"

"That we're doing this again," Kingsley said. "You want something for your whole life, and you get so used to wanting it, you don't know how to get used to having it."

Kingsley stood at the bedpost nearest the door, as if he couldn't bring himself to accept he was here, really here, an invited guest, a wanted guest.

Søren came to him. "I sent you away too many times. I shut you out too long. I wouldn't blame you if you hated me, if you walked out the door right now to punish me."

"Would it punish you?"

"I can't think of anything I want less right now than for you to leave."

Kingsley met his eyes, his steel-gray eyes and saw the truth shining in them, turning them silver. Søren was afraid that Kingsley might walk out—that this was too little, too late.

Kingsley went to the door, and paused at the threshold—he was a sadist himself, after all—before shutting the bedroom door.

The clicking of the brass bolt into place was one of the more erotic sounds he'd ever heard.

"I knew you weren't going to leave," Søren said, grinning slightly. "Come here."

Søren pointed to the old oval country rug at the foot of the bed. Kingsley committed the rug's colors and placement to memory, as he did with the entire room—the four-poster bed, the tops of the posts so tall they nearly brushed the ceiling. The quilt, downy white. The leather armchair and small side table, where a brass reading lamp sat.

Kingsley took his place on the rug. No one, unless they had submitted to someone they loved and respected, could ever understand the beautiful freedom of taking orders given by someone you trusted with your heart and your body. Nora had the best explanation for it. He remembered a lazy night at The 8th Circle, sitting around a table with Griffin and a few others, when one of the club's dominatrixes demanded Nora explain why she still sometimes submitted to Søren, why she'd take the servant's role to a man when she was born to be a master.

And Nora had said, "Imagine you know a guy—an investment banker, maybe—and you know that even if you handed over every penny of your fortune and watched him walk away with it...that when he came back a day later, or a week later, it would be with double your money, triple even. Imagine giving up all you have to someone, knowing you're going to get it back and then some. If you knew that guy, you'd love him, wouldn't you? Even if you didn't love him, you'd love him. You'd kiss his fucking hands, wouldn't you? You'd kiss his fucking feet."

The dominatrix who'd challenged Nora conceded defeat and kissed Nora's boot in penance. She was right. No denying. And if Kingsley hadn't been ordered to stand there on the rug by the bed, he might have dropped to his knees and kissed Søren's fucking hands, his fucking feet.

Søren lifted his hand and cupped the back of Kingsley's neck. "What do you want from me tonight? I'm in a giving mood."

Kingsley knew there was no right or wrong answer to that question. It wasn't a sincere query, just a way to make Kingsley squirm a little, embarrass him by making him talk about his fantasies. It took a lot to embarrass Kingsley, but Søren's steady gaze on him—his waiting, watching, judging regard—always turned him back into a nervous teenager, terrified of saying the wrong thing.

"The usual, I guess. Sex and kink, and it's all very hot and intense, et cetera, et cetera."

"Et cetera, et cetera?"

"I'll leave the 'et cetera' to you."

"Sex and kink, et cetera." Søren's tone was stern but amused. Professorial, like a teacher trying to find a kernel of sense somewhere in a very stupid pupil's reply. "Could you possibly be more specific?"

He could, actually. Kingsley remembered

who he was then—not a skinny, scared teenager anymore but a grown man, a man other men were rightly afraid of.

And he knew exactly what he wanted.

Søren's bed was beautiful, two hundred or more years old. Oak with hand-carved spindles. No surprise that after two hundred years, the wood was scuffed and scratched. It wasn't time that had left its mark on the bed, but rather Søren and Nora. Kingsley had watched with his own eyes, lying on those pillows, as Søren had flogged her while she was cuffed to the bedpost. Flogged her then fucked her. All those scratches, those gouges, those grooves, they were all souvenirs of her nights here.

"You have gouges and scratches all over your bed," he said. "Did you ever notice that?"

"I've noticed," Søren said, touching a deep dent in the footboard. "If I ever leave, I'll have to have the bed refinished."

"All these are hers," Kingsley said. "You tie her up here and flog her and whip her and beat her. None of them are mine. I've never left so much as a scratch."

"Would you like to leave a scratch or two on my bed?"

"I'd like you to fuck me so hard the bedposts break off, but I'll settle for one or two of these of my own." He stroked the marks left by handcuffs, by snap hooks, by desperate fingernails.

Kingsley wanted to leave his mark there, too. Something permanent. Something left behind that declared to the world, KINGSLEY WAS HERE.

"Let's leave some marks then." Søren brushed his lips lightly over Kingsley's and whispered two words that left Kingsley breathless.

"Deep ones."

CHAPTER FIVE

SØREN ORDERED HIM TO UNDRESS. Kingsley obeyed, but slowly. He wanted everything to be slow tonight. No rush. No hurry. Make the evening last as long as possible.

He took off his suit jacket, tossed it over the back of the chair. Then the button-down, deftly freeing one button at a time. Meanwhile, Søren had unlocked the big steamer trunk. Hidden under the neatly folded sheets and quilts were all of Søren's toys. Floggers. Whips. Handcuffs. Misery sticks. Leather cuffs. Snap hooks. Spreader bars. Ankle cuffs.

Kingsley grew more and more aroused as the seconds passed and the silence grew heavy with possibility. Shoes off. Socks off. Trousers off. Then there was nothing left to take off.

Søren emerged from the chest with a ring. A large metal ring. Definitely not a cock ring, unless the cock in question belonged to a bull elephant.

"What's that?" Kingsley asked.

"You wanted to leave marks on my bed," Søren said, placing the metal hoop over the top of the wooden spindle, where it stayed like a ring tossed onto a peg during a carnival game. "Your own marks. She can't reach that high. I think you can."

Søren picked up two leather wrist cuffs. Kingsley was six feet tall, but even so, he would have to stretch if he were cuffed to that ring. The higher his hands were tied, the less secure footing he would have, and the more vulnerable he would be—no doubt precisely why Søren had thought of it.

Søren casually tossed the cuffs onto the bed, then unbuttoned his shirt. He threw it at Kingsley, who knew what to do. He neatly folded the shirt and laid it over the back of the chair, and just like that, he was sixteen again. This was how it had been. This is how it would be. Only this time, he hoped, without the terrible ending.

From the toy box, Søren removed a flogger with oiled leather tails. Kingsley closed his eyes, breathed a silent "*Merde.*" Oiled leather was bad. Oiled leather meant sharp, stinging sensations. Oiled leather was not for beginners, because oiled leather could cause serious pain.

"You don't use that on Nora, do you?" Kingsley asked.

"Never. Though she's been threatened with it. Keeps her in line, more or less."

He gave Kingsley a wicked, almost demonic grin. Then Søren moved closer, pressed his bare chest to Kingsley's. The skin to skin contact was delicious, electric. Kingsley's cock stiffened. It ached for touching and sucking, but the night had only just begun. Relief was hours away.

The flogger hung on Søren's wrist by the strap, and when he cupped Kingsley's neck lightly—and then not so lightly—Kingsley felt the tails gently brushing his naked back.

"I would never use this on Eleanor," Søren said, meeting Kingsley's eyes. "I've been saving it for you."

"What did I do to deserve the honor?"

"You showed up."

Søren's mouth found his again, kissed him deeply but too briefly. He raised Kingsley's wrist to his lips and bit him hard, over the pulse point, hard enough to break the skin. Just a nip of teeth, but it sent a jolt of sharp pain through his entire body. The blood welled up, not much more than a pinprick, but Søren's pupils dilated at the sight of it until there was more black in his eyes than gray.

Slowly, Søren lowered Kingsley's hand and placed it flat against the center of his chest. Kingsley could feel Søren's steady, strong heartbeat against his palm. Then Søren picked up one leather cuff and wrapped it around Kingsley's wrist, buckling it with his quick, agile fingers... fingers that had done this so many times, on so many nights, that surely he could have done it in his sleep. The leather cuff abraded the small bite wound on Kingsley's wrist. With every flinch, every twist, he would feel it again.

Which was, of course, precisely why Søren did it.

When both wrists were cuffed, Søren took out a snap hook and ordered Kingsley to face the bedpost and raise his arms. He could just barely reach the ring, standing on his toes. Søren, four inches taller, had no difficulty strapping him in and stretching him further in the process. Kingsley clenched his teeth as the muscles of his arms and back went taut and lengthened as if pulled on a rack.

In a proper flogging, the top warms the submissive up with a light start. The pain goes slowly and gently from a one to a two, a two to a four. Gradually, carefully, and with respect.

But this was Kingsley, a whore for pain.

And this was Søren, a man who made pain sluts cry for their mothers.

The first strike was brutal. Brutal and beautiful, just like the man who delivered it. Kingsley was caught so off guard by the pain that he cried out. When no second strike immediately followed, he knew he was in trouble.

"We're in the rectory of a Catholic church, Kingsley," Søren reminded him in his most insufferable tone. "Let's keep it down, shall we? Or do I need to gag you?"

Kingsley gave that question serious thought. Oiled leather flogger? No way to move into or away from the pain?

"Better gag me," he said.

Søren silently retrieved a gag from his toy box and tied it around Kingsley's head.

"Shall I continue?" Søren asked in his ear. "Oh, you're gagged. You can't answer. I'll take your silence for consent."

Kingsley's silence *was* his consent. His presence was his consent. When it came to Søren, Kingsley's existence was his consent.

"I promise I'll stop if you pass out from blood loss," Søren added.

This was a joke. At least Kingsley hoped it was. With Søren, one could never be sure...

The second strike was as hard and as harsh as the first. A line of fire burned across Kingsley's back. Then the third strike, and the fire went wild.

Kingsley braced himself as well as he could against the bedpost, shoulder to oak, and let the fire rain down on him. On his shoulders, on his sides, on his ass, thighs; even the tender skin on the back of his knees wasn't spared. The sensation went beyond stinging and burning to a place of absolute obliterating conflagration. If someone had doused him in gasoline and thrown a match on him, he might not notice. His body was a sacrificial bonfire and Søren the god for whom he burned. Everything turned to ash in the fire: His fears for the future. His dark memories of the past. His ego. His needs. His wants. His hopes. He was nothing but a body.

Then it was over, the cool air kissing his raw skin. He hung limp from the bedpost, covered in sweat and shivering, panting against the gag.

Søren pushed his bare chest against Kingsley's back. Kingsley almost passed out from the sudden wave of pain as Søren's sweat stung his wounded flesh.

But it was worth it. God, was it worth it when Søren wrapped his arms around his stomach, put his lips to his ear, and said, "Thank you."

Søren kissed him on the back of the neck where the strap of the gag had rubbed his skin red. He kissed Kingsley's shoulders, still burning, and the back of his head. Søren's lips dug hard into Kingsley's skin like he was close to coming, and it was true—he could feel his lover's powerful erection against his back.

This was one of those rare and perfect moments when Kingsley felt Søren's need, so much greater than his own. No matter how much Kingsley wanted it—and he did want it, beyond love or money—Søren *needed* it, like food, water. Like air. And if you needed air and didn't have it, wouldn't you put your lips to the ear of the man who'd given it to you to whisper your thanks?

Søren finally unbuckled the gag and pulled it gently out of Kingsley's mouth before dropping it onto the rug. Then he reached up and unhooked the snap hooks. Kingsley's arms fell down to his sides like deadweight. His knees nearly buckled. But he didn't have to worry that he'd fall. Søren had him. Kingsley leaned back against him, resting there. Søren's arms were around him, his chin on Kingsley's shoulder.

"Happy now?" Søren asked softly, laughter in his voice. "Now that you left your mark on the bed?"

Kingsley opened his tired eyes and saw the steel ring had cut gouges into the top of the bed-post, gouges so deep they'd exposed the pale wood underneath the dark stain and varnish.

Blissfully, he smiled.

"Very, very happy."

CHAPTER SIX

KINGSLEY STOOD ON HIS FEET, steady again, and turned around, kissing Søren with hunger and need. But kisses weren't enough to satisfy the craving. He went onto his knees and kissed and licked Søren's bare and beautiful stomach, tasting the sweat.

As much as Kingsley wanted his cock and wanted it right then, he made himself slow down. Made it last and last. If he'd learned anything this year, it was that everything could change in an instant. Everything could, with a knock on the door or a call on the phone, just...disappear.

Slowly, he opened Søren's black trousers and lowered them down past his jutting hipbones. Kingsley had to bite them, or he would die right there on the floor of the rectory's bedroom, which would undoubtedly put Søren in an awkward position. So he did them both a favor and bit them, nipping the pale flesh with the tips of his teeth. Søren flinched and caught his breath.

Søren had a sadist's respect for pain. A connoisseur of it, really, and happy to be on the receiving end if and when the pain was inflicted on him by an overly enthusiastic submissive.

Søren was hard, his cock stiff and thick. Kingsley slid his palm up the shaft and wrapped his fingers around it, holding it as he bit Søren's left hip a little harder. Not too hard. Just hard enough to leave teeth marks and a bruise that Nora might see in a day or two. Kingsley was in a mood to leave his mark on Søren tonight—his bed, his body. He'd tattoo his name on the man's soul if he could find his way to it.

Kingsley brought the tip of Søren's penis to his lips, licked it, and circled it with his tongue. Then he slowly....slowly....slowly....drew it into his mouth. He held it by the base and took as much of it as he could. He tasted salt again, but not sweat. He forced his jaw to relax so he could take as much as possible into his throat, and once it was there he pumped his mouth around it.

Søren's hands found Kingsley's hair and stroked it, then gripped it to hold him in place.

He tilted Kingsley's head back slightly, and Kingsley let it happen without protest or struggle. He let Søren use his mouth as he knelt there and took it. This was what he'd craved for years, this giving up of self and will and autonomy. It wasn't always good to be a king. There was much to be said for being a servant, especially with this man as his master.

Kingsley opened his eyes and looked up.

Søren was astride him practically, his legs parted and his hands holding Kingsley's head right where he wanted it. His bare chest glistened in the lamplight, his tight stomach muscles moving with each of his breaths. His eyes were closed as if in prayer.

Kingsley slid his hands up Søren's thighs and to his back, his long and muscled back. He dug his fingers into the tender skin, wanting to draw Søren deeper into his mouth.

Søren gasped—a sound as wild and welcome as sudden thunder on a stifling summer night—and released into Kingsley's mouth. Søren's come filled his throat, and he had to swallow fast or choke. He swallowed every drop and licked his lips when it was done. Søren stood over him, hands still in Kingsley's hair.

Kingsley leaned his head against Søren's hip and rested there. When Søren laughed softly, Kingsley looked up.

"I didn't plan on doing that," Søren said.

"Good," Kingsley said, resting his head again on the center of Søren's stomach. "I liked making you lose control."

"Doesn't happen very often." Søren ran his fingers through Kingsley's hair. "Did you do that on purpose?"

Kingsley sat back on his knees and watched as Søren zipped up his trousers. "Suck your cock like my life depended on it? Yes."

"Make me come."

Kingsley shrugged. "If I didn't make you come now, I knew you'd fuck me. And I didn't want you to fuck me now. I wanted you to fuck me later."

"Usually you want me to fuck you immediately."

"I suppose I'm in the mood to take things slower tonight. I don't want it to be over too soon."

"No matter what, you can stay as long as you like."

Hearing those words made him feel almost as good as swallowing every drop of Søren's come had.

"I told you...I'm still getting used to us being together again. I may never get used to it," Kingsley said.

Søren reached down and stroked Kingsley's now-swollen bottom lip. His face was solemn, his eyes stern.

"Get used to it."

CHAPTER SEVEN

Søren sent Kingsley downstairs to find a bottle of red wine and two glasses. While in the kitchen, Kingsley checked his phone and found Juliette had sent him a photo of her and Nora at the theater in their box seats, both women looking elegant in their evening gowns. They'd be out late, so Kingsley didn't have to hurry home. Juliette was always happy to have a night off from his hovering attentions. Yesterday he'd tried to convince her to move their bedroom to the ground floor so she wouldn't have to climb the stairs. To that she said, "I'm pregnant, not dying." And that was the end of that.

He started up the stairs with the wine. From down the hall, he heard Søren on the phone. Kingsley walked quietly to the office and peeked inside. Søren was standing behind his desk, phone to his ear. While Kingsley had been downstairs, Søren had changed into a soft gray t-shirt and black and gray plaid flannel pants.

How did he still look like a priest even in his pajamas?

Søren waved him inside the office.

"Did she ever wake up?" Søren was saying to whoever was on the other end of the line. Then a pause. "I'm so sorry, John. Your mother was an incredible woman." Another pause. "Go home. Get some sleep. Your mother's not there anymore. The nurses will take good care of her." Pause. "No, I wouldn't tell the girls tonight. Let them sleep. Tell them after breakfast tomorrow morning." Another long pause. "I'll be over at ten. You don't have to do anything tonight but rest up for tomorrow. Everything else can wait."

With quiet compassion and the subtle note of command in his voice, Søren counseled the man. It was always so strange to witness this side of Kingsley's enigmatic lover. How did he reconcile such compassion and kindness with his sadism? Kingsley wondered if Søren had invisible grooves on the bottom of his feet from walking that tightrope his entire adult life.

"John, you know as well as I do that if your mother were still here, she would tell you to go home and take care of her granddaughters. Put them first, and you'll get through this." Pause. "Yes, Diane and I will see you in the morning. We'll take care of everything."

Another pause. Søren said goodnight and hung up the phone, setting it down lightly on the desk.

Søren met Kingsley's eyes. "Parishioner lost

his mother. He'd taken her into the ER on Tuesday, when she was having a stroke. He said he couldn't bring himself to just leave her there in the hospital with strangers."

"She's dead."

"He knows, but it hasn't quite sunk in yet. He just needed someone with a little authority to give him permission to do what he already wanted to do."

"You're his dominant."

Søren softly laughed, winced. "I admit that thought has occurred to me on more than one occasion when it comes to my parishioners." Søren accepted a glass from Kingsley and took a deep drink of wine. "I needed that, thank you."

"You're a good priest."

"Not as good as they deserve," he said with a shrug, settling down behind his desk. "But I do my best. I need to call Diane about John's mother. Give me two minutes, and you'll have my full attention again."

"No rush. I'll let you—"

"You can stay," Søren said, picking up his phone again.

Kingsley decided he would do that. He'd rarely had a reason to go into Søren's office. In fact, he'd probably been in this room only half a dozen times in the seventeen years Søren had been at Sacred Heart. Although he vaguely recalled a time they'd crawled out of the large picture window with the bench seat behind his desk, the easiest route to the roof of the rectory.

Window to ivy-covered iron trellis to roof. Was that how they'd gotten back in again? No, they'd broken the trellis, he remembered. The rest of the memory escaped him.

As Søren spoke with his secretary, Kingsley studied the office. Seemingly nothing had changed since the last time he'd been in here—and it had been years. Years and years. The walls were painted a creamy white and the hardwood floor was covered by a large faded Persian rug that had once been blue and gold, he would guess, but was now a dull gray and an even duller yellow. Floor-to-ceiling built-in bookcases held Bibles and dense theological tomes, some in Latin and Greek, languages that Søren read as comfortably as he read English and French. The desk was large, but not grand. Honey-colored oak, like an old-fashioned schoolteacher's desk with an antique brass lamp on top. None of the decor seemed particularly "Søren," and Kingsley assumed everything in the office had been here when he'd moved in and would stay here if he ever moved out. Except Kingsley couldn't imagine Søren anywhere but in Wakefield, celebrating mass six days a week, presiding over funerals and weddings, and coaching a ragtag team of co-ed intramural soccer players—the Sacred Heart Attacks, their mascot a cartoon heart brandishing a broadsword.

The Heart Attacks' second-place trophy from the 2010 church league tournament was perched on a small metal box on the shelf.

Fucking First Presbyterian had taken the championship. Again.

The trophy wasn't the only addition to the office, though. Hanging on the wall was a small round sampler Kingsley hadn't seen before.

TRUTH MAKES LOVE POSSIBLE; BUT LOVE MAKES TRUTH BEARABLE.

— ACHBISHOP ROWAN WILLIAMS.

A gift from a parishioner to Søren, Kingsley guessed, reading the tiny sewn-on letters at the bottom: TO FR. MS FROM KJ.

Søren got off the phone with Diane and sat in his office chair, swiveling it to face Kingsley who stood at the bookcase by the window.

"Sorry," he said, sitting back in the chair. "Priests don't work nine to five."

"It's fine," Kingsley said. "Really." He turned and sat down on the window bench, though the glass was cold and there was nothing to see outside but the dark, icy branches of an elm tree. "Who is KJ?" Kingsley asked, nodding toward the sampler on the wall.

"KJ? Oh, Katherine Jensen. She's in the choir, does embroidery in her free time."

"Does she have a crush on you?"

"She's ninety-one. But yes, I think she does."

Kingsley smiled. "You put our trophy in here."

"I was hiding it in shame," Søren said, feigning disgust. "I will never forgive First Presbyterian for beating us again. You know they cheated."

"How?"

"By having better players on their team than we did."

Kingsley sipped his wine and set his glass down. "What's in the box?"

"Which box?"

"The locked one. Under the trophy."

Søren glanced over his shoulder at the box, and his eyes were different when he looked back. "Just letters."

"In a lockbox."

"They're from Elizabeth," Søren said. "Old letters from when I was in school."

Elizabeth, Søren's sister with whom he shared a troubled past. She'd been abused by their father as a little girl. When she was twelve and Søren eleven, she'd instigated an incestuous abusive relationship with him. Her own brother. Søren had said before how difficult it was to even be in the same room with her, that it brought back disturbing memories.

"I shouldn't have asked," Kingsley said.

"You can ask me anything," Søren said gently, as if he were talking to a scared child about to make a difficult confession. "You know that, don't you? If it's something I can answer, I will."

"Really?" Kingsley shook his head. "Forgive me for being skeptical. I feel like you've been keeping yourself a secret from me for years."

"I know," Søren said with a solemn nod. "I was. In my mind, I'd convinced myself I was protecting you. I think the truth is, I was protecting myself just as much, if not more. But I'm trying to be more honest with all of us. If you want to know something, ask it."

"You'll regret saying that."

Søren grinned. "Try me."

CHAPTER EIGHT

Try him? That blond monster was as arrogant as he was beautiful. Kingsley would show him.

"All right. First question. Where did you get your pajamas? Is there a pajama catalog just for priests?"

"You like them? Eleanor got them for me. And red ones covered in candy canes, too."

"They make those in your size?"

Søren picked up his wine glass. "Apparently so."

"They're very cute."

"Thank you. I always wanted to be cute." He took a drink. "That's your question?"

"I have more."

Søren held out his hand, palm open. "Ask away."

"Why do you keep your sister's letters?"

Søren sat back again, exhaled hard. "The pajama question was much easier to answer. I've wanted to burn them many times. However, since Elizabeth writes about my father's abuse in them, destroying them would feel like destroying evidence. Stuart Ballard—"

"Who?"

"The priest who's my confessor—he suggested I put them in a locked box, throw away the key, and set them on a shelf where I might see them every day until I'm used to them, and they no longer hold any power over me. It's called exposure therapy. Seems to have worked. Now they're just letters in a box. They have some sentimental value, too, I suppose. Apart from the occasional threatening letter from my father, no one ever wrote to me at school. I felt completely abandoned there. Finally, after two years, Elizabeth somehow found out where I'd been sent, and she started writing to me in secret. The first letter I received from her was a godsend. I can't tell you how crushing my loneliness was there." He smiled. "Until a certain French whore and masochist came along and changed my life."

Happiness again, pure happiness, potent as cocaine, hit Kingsley's brainstem and shot through his whole body.

"Does Nora know that you have those letters?"

"I don't think so. She's never asked. I've asked her not to ask. Shockingly, she's obeyed."

"There's a small horrible part of me that's happy I know, and she doesn't."

"I don't think that's particularly horrible, just understandable, considering. Any other questions?"

"Tell me something else she doesn't know." Kingsley grinned, feeling deliciously evil.

"Something Eleanor doesn't know? Let's see... Well, this is hardly a deep, dark secret, but I didn't tell her that I was recently offered a theology professorship at the Gregorian in Rome."

Kingsley's eyes widened. "When was that?"

"About a month ago. They wanted me to start next summer."

"Rome?"

"Rome."

"And you told them no?" If Søren wouldn't leave Sacred Heart for a cushy teaching position in Rome, he'd never... Kingsley pushed the rest of that thought aside.

"After everything we've just been through, I could hardly ask Eleanor and you and Juliette to uproot yourselves and come with me, could I? And I wasn't going to leave without you."

Kingsley ignored a pang of guilt. "Did you want to take the job?"

"I miss teaching. Being the only priest at a parish this size is exhausting. In a perfect world, I'd be teaching, but we don't live in a perfect world."

"If you weren't planning on taking it, why keep it from Nora?"

Søren met his eyes briefly, then looked away. "She's fragile right now," he said. "Doing better than most people would after what she went through, but she's not quite there yet. I've lost count of the times I've called her over the years and said I needed her to come over and be with me. Never once has she called to say she needed me."

"And now?"

"Three times in as many months. Which isn't many on paper but it's a lot for her. Most of the time, she swears she's fine, and I believe her. But sometimes when she's alone...sometimes she just can't be alone."

"You like that, don't you? That she needs you now."

"It's gratifying, yes. I wish the cause were different, but since we're being honest, it means..." He paused and smiled. "It means *everything* to me. Just mentioning to her the possibility I might go away—even if I'm not planning to, which I'm not—it would worry her. And worry is the last thing she needs, especially since she's starting to get back to her old self." He smiled. "Any other brutally personal questions?"

"One million. Give or take."

"How about one more, and then we go to bed? Surely we could save the other 999,999 for tomorrow?"

"What's something you never told me? Something about us."

Søren raised his arms and clasped his hands behind his head, the picture of deep contemplation. Kingsley would have killed to be inside that blond head, seeing all those memories flashing across his mind's eye like a montage from a black-and-white film.

"I got you a Christmas present," Søren said.

"That's not a secret. We get each other Christmas presents every year."

"Not this year. Back then."

"When we were in school?"

Søren nodded. "By the time it finally arrived, you were already gone and not coming back."

Kingsley sat up straighter, looked at him. "What was it?"

"You used to brag that you were scouted by Paris Saint-Germain FC."

"I had been, I swear."

"I believed you. That's why I wrote Elizabeth and asked her to buy a PSG football shirt when she was in Paris for Christmas that year and ship it to me. She did, but the post was slow, and it didn't arrive until a week after you were gone. It sat wrapped in brown paper with twine —the only wrapping paper we had at school— until the end of the term. Sat on my dresser taunting me every day, reminding me you'd left and weren't coming back. When I went to France to look for you after the term ended, I took it with me, but I never found you. When you join the Jesuits, you have to give up all your worldly possessions. That shirt was the very last thing I gave away. A homeless man was begging for change across the street from the building. He looked about your size."

Kingsley stared at Søren and didn't speak at first. In the silence, a branch from the frozen elm tree outside scratched the frosted window. The wind blew softly, but he felt it creeping through the cracks in the old and drafty cottage.

The moment was already becoming a memory, one of his most important, one that would keep him warm in any season, safe in any storm.

There was nothing you could say to a confession like that, that the man you loved more than your own life had clung to a scrap of fabric for months and months and had only let go at the very last second, like a bride turning back one last time before walking down the aisle to make sure the man she truly loved wasn't coming to claim her. Or like Lot's wife looking back at Sodom before being turned into a pillar of salt.

Since there was nothing to say, Kingsley said nothing. He went over to Søren, sitting in his office chair, and he went down onto his knees on the rug in front of him and rested his head in Søren's lap.

Søren put his hand in Kingsley's hair and just held his head against his thigh. Kingsley inhaled deeply and smelled the scent of winter, the scent of trees encased in ice, but earthy and bursting with life within.

"I have a problem," Kingsley said. "I've gotten used to it."

Søren laughed softly. "It shouldn't be a problem. I told you, it's not going away."

No, maybe not, Kingsley thought. Maybe Søren's love wasn't going away.

But Kingsley was.

CHAPTER NINE

"Come to bed," Søren said, and Kingsley obeyed.

Kingsley went first, and Søren walked behind him. Once inside the bedroom, Søren shut the door. Kingsley heard the click of the door latch, his new favorite sound.

Talking was over. All the secrets that would be told that night had been told. As soon as the door shut and the world was outside it, Søren took Kingsley's face in his hands, possessively, forced his head back, and kissed him like he owned him. He did own him, had every right to him.

Quickly, roughly, Kingsley's clothes were stripped from his body. Buttons unbuttoned. Shirt tossed aside. He was hard already from the kiss, but his penis stiffened even more when Søren pushed him onto his back on the bed and crawled on top of him.

Even six months pregnant, Juliette was light as a feather compared to the sheer breathtaking mass of the six-foot-four man on top of him. Was there anything like being kissed while fighting for air that made one feel more used? More owned?

The quilt was soft against Kingsley's skin and cradled his body as he sank into the bed.

White hand-made quilt, antique bed, light from an old brass lamp. It was like making love in another time, another world, a world so removed from the real one that Kingsley was able to forget that their nights like this were numbered.

Søren rose up on his knees, straddling Kingsley's waist. "Do you want to leave marks on the bed?" he asked.

Kingsley answered, "I would carve my name across your headboard if you let me. I'd leave teeth marks in your footboard. I'd let you bleed me into the mattress so deep the stain would never come out. I'd..."

Kingsley paused as Søren's eyebrow reached his hairline.

"So that's a yes," Søren said.

Søren left the bed to go to his steamer trunk, his box of tricks. While he was gone, Kingsley moved fully onto the bed, lying in the middle, head on a pillow. Søren returned with two sets of steel handcuffs. Two? Søren straddled him again, putting one set on each wrist. The snapping of the lock into place and the cool touch of the metal on his already tender wrists made Kingsley desperately hard. His cock throbbed, wanting to be touched. Once the cuffs were on,

Søren turned him onto his stomach. Kingsley lay there, prone and defenseless as Søren cuffed each wrist to a bedpost, his arms locked in a wide V.

Kingsley relaxed at once, surrendering himself entirely to the grip of the cuffs. He closed his eyes and rested his face against the quilt, soft from a thousand washings and smelling clean as a spring dawn.

His back was covered in bruises from the earlier beating, and even the slightest touch hurt. So that was all Søren administered at first, light touches on his tender back. His large and heavy hand stroked the wounds, lighting them up like signal fires with every touch.

"It wouldn't be right," Søren said, his tone quiet and gentle, "to put bruises on top of your bruises. It wouldn't be right at all, really. But it will be very, very enjoyable."

Not would be. *Will* be.

Kingsley registered the switch in verb tense at the exact moment Søren brought the short crop down onto his back. Not only onto his back, but directly onto a fresh bruise. Kingsley buried his face into the quilt to muffle his cries. The pain was staggering. Tears filled his eyes, and he pulled hard enough on the cuffs that bound him that he could feel the metal digging into the wood.

Then it was over, and Kingsley panted against the pillow, his back as hot and throbbing as his cock. Cool air soothed his raw skin, but the respite was brief. Something touched his bruises again, and Kingsley cried out softly. He felt it again and knew what it was this time. Not a hand. Not the crop. Søren was kissing his back, kissing his bruises. Kissing them softly, but even Søren's softest kisses caused him pain. Those were his favorite kisses, the ones that hurt.

Søren kissed a wandering path up Kingsley's body from the small of his back to his sides, his ribs, between his shoulders, and then his neck. Søren was naked. Kingsley felt Søren's cock pushing against the back of his thigh. A dizzying sensation, to be desired by this man.

He felt Søren's hands slide up his arms. Then the handcuffs were off and tossed onto the floor with a metallic clatter. Kingsley's body was loose and listless after the rush of pain. He let Søren turn him onto his back. He returned to full awareness at the moment when Søren laid down a black towel onto the bed, then picked up a small scalpel off the bedside table. No words were spoken, but Kingsley's heart pounded loud enough he could hear it beating in his ears.

"Hold very still," Søren said, his voice tender and soothing. "I don't want to hurt you."

Søren was going to cut him with a scalpel, but he didn't want to hurt him. Only to a sadist and the masochist who loved him did such a breach of logic make any sense. He meant that he didn't want to hurt Kingsley unintentionally. He did, of course, want to hurt him—entirely on purpose and in exactly the manner he desired. That was Søren.

Kingsley, as ordered, did not move.

The chosen spot was on Kingsley's hip, in that hollow of sensitive skin near the bone.

"You left your marks," Søren said, head down and leaning over Kingsley's hip. "Now I'll leave mine."

Kingsley watched Søren with hooded eyes, devouring the sight of his lover's tender concentration. The beauty of a sadist at work. The intensity in his steel-colored eyes. The steadiness of his hand. A lock of silver-blond hair falling over his forehead. The lips parting in pleasure as the skin slit under the sharpest edge of the knife...

A small cut, but precise and in the shape of an S. Blood welled to the surface. Søren's pupils dilated and took over his eyes.

"Are you all right?" Søren asked.

"I have never been better."

Truly, only Søren could wield kisses like a knife and a knife like a kiss.

Everything happened fast after that. Søren moved Kingsley onto his side, opened him with wet fingers slick with lubricant. And then he was inside him, moving deep with long strokes. Side by side, Søren's chest to Kingsley's back and his hand clutching the bleeding hip, four legs entwined, breaths ragged and rushed.

Slow thrusts. Deep thrusts. Kingsley felt them all the way into the aching core of him. Søren's hand on Kingsley's cock. A wet hand wrapped around a thick cock. Stroking in time with the thrusts so that Kingsley felt overwhelmed by pleasure, pleasure in and pleasure out. He wanted to come more than he wanted to breathe, but even more he wanted to hold back and come with Søren.

He shut his eyes tight and breathed shallow breaths, even as his climax built. With his own hand on himself, he could have held back easier, controlled his arousal. But with Søren's hand, so firm and grasping, it took herculean effort to hold back. The muscles of his stomach tightened painfully even as his hips worked into the hand that held him, and the cock inside him speared him completely.

"Come," Søren ordered into his ear, and Kingsley couldn't disobey. His back bowed and he let go, coming in spurts onto the white sheets even as Søren pounded into him with rough thrusts Kingsley barely registered through the wild haze of orgasm. As soon as he was empty, he was filled again. Søren came inside him as Kingsley lay limp and spent on the bed.

Then it was over, and they lay together, breathing together, bound together.

Søren slowly held out his hand and showed it to Kingsley. He saw the blood from the cut on his hip, staining the fingers and palm.

"It looks like my blood is your blood," Kingsley said.

And Søren replied, "Your blood is my blood."

Kingsley closed his eyes and asked himself how he could possibly leave this behind.

He didn't know how, only that he would.

CHAPTER TEN

SLOWLY THEY DISENTANGLED from each other. Søren pulled on his black flannel pajama pants and left Kingsley naked and spent on the bed. Shortly, Søren returned, his hands freshly washed—no more blood—carrying a first-aid kit.

Søren gently swabbed the cut on his hip, then applied ointment and gauze.

"You know," Kingsley said, never able to resist a chance to taunt Søren, "the famous Mistress Nora uses Snoopy brand Band-Aids when she cuts you up in her dungeon."

"Yes, well, the famous Mistress Nora is slightly demented, I hear."

"That's what we boys pay her for."

"Yes, I've heard that, too."

Kingsley smiled as Søren snapped the first-aid kit shut. "You're handling it better," he said. "Her work. When did that happen?"

"I'm still not thrilled about it, but how could I deny her what I won't deny myself?"

"Easily. You'd done it for years. So what changed?"

Søren looked at him. "You were in that room. We all were. You know what changed."

Everything. Everything changed and there was no going back.

"How could I deny her anything now?" Søren said. "All that matters is that she's alive and safe. And you."

Søren slipped out of his clothes again, turned off the lamp, and slid into bed with him. Without thinking, Kingsley curled up against him and laid his head on Søren's stomach.

"Don't let me fall asleep," Kingsley said. "I want to be home by midnight."

"What happens at midnight?"

"Juliette will want crêpes."

"You make her crêpes at midnight? Midnight crêpes?"

"She's six months pregnant with my baby. If she wants crêpes at midnight and blood oranges at dawn and a rack of lamb for lunch, she gets it."

"Maybe I want midnight crêpes."

"Are you pregnant with my child?"

"Not at the moment."

"Then make your own fucking crêpes."

Søren's stomach moved under Kingsley's head, rolling like a wave as he quietly laughed.

In the silence, Kingsley asked a question he'd been afraid to ask before. "Are you all right?"

Søren took a deep breath before answering. "Strangely, I think I'm better now than I was before. And Eleanor will be, too, eventually. Sometimes she has nightmares, and so do I, but there's a new honesty between us, a new certainty. Neither of us are content to wait for happiness anymore. She and I wanted to be together. We are together. You and I wanted to be together. So here we are—together."

"It does change your priorities, realizing you could die, doesn't it?"

"How did it change yours?"

Dangerous question. One Kingsley wasn't prepared to answer yet.

"I'm leaving your bed to go and make crêpes for Jules," he said. "Does that answer your question?"

"You're doing that because she's pregnant, not because of what happened to us. What's going on?"

Kingsley raised his head, saw Søren looking at him. "What are you asking?"

"For weeks now, you've been acting differently. And tonight...when did you start taking pictures of my church? Of the trees? You hugged Maxine earlier like you might never see her again. And all evening you've been asking me to be honest with you, which makes me wonder if you're not being completely honest with me. Is there something going on you aren't telling me about?"

As much as Kingsley wanted to stay there, resting his head on Søren's stomach for another hour or century, he slowly sat up and gathered the sheets around him.

Søren switched the lamp back on and sat up, too, back against the headboard, white quilt at his waist. "Kingsley?"

"Something happened on my birthday," he began. "You know how I said I didn't want a party."

"I remember."

"All I wanted was to be alone with Juliette all evening. She had a meal delivered from my favorite French restaurant, and then all we did was curl up in my sitting room and talk and read. Then I heard something. People were pounding on the door, yelling my name. Juliette was scared. But you know who it was?"

"Who?"

"People I've known for years. They were dressed up, drunk, ready for a party. And I couldn't get rid of them fast enough."

Søren smiled, looked relieved. "Is that it? You've realized you're over your playboy ways?"

"It's more than that. I was scared. Me. And the reason they were pounding on the door was because I had locked it. I never used to lock the doors. I didn't want anyone thinking I was scared. But now I am. All the time. Day and night. Juliette carries pepper spray wherever she goes. I'd carry a gun with me, if she'd let me. But I have them in the house, which I'm under orders to get rid of the second the baby is born."

"You're about to be a father. Things have to change."

"I read something a long time ago that's stayed with me. Tacitus, the Roman historian, said, 'Great empires are not maintained by timidity.' I have never been as happy in my life as I am now. And I've never been so afraid."

"Are you afraid your empire is going to fall?"

"Fuck my empire. Burn it to the ground. I don't want it anymore."

"What do you want, then?"

"I want to take Juliette and the baby and move to the other side of the world. That's what I want." He paused, met Søren's eyes, and said the hardest words he'd ever said. "And that's what we're going to do."

CHAPTER ELEVEN

Søren stared. The silence was so profound that Kingsley heard a tree limb scratching the roof.

"You're leaving New York," Søren finally said. "You and Juliette."

Kingsley nodded.

"For how long?"

"Forever." Before Søren could ask another question, Kingsley started to explain himself. "We're not safe here. I made too many enemies. I've crossed the mafia. I've pissed off the police, politicians... I know the secrets of too many powerful people. Next time someone knocks on my door in the middle of the night, they might have a gun in their hand instead of a bottle of champagne. I have to think of Jules. I have to think of the baby. You told that man tonight on the phone he had to put his children first. That's all I'm trying to do."

Another silence, loud enough that Kingsley

heard the quiet ping of the carriage clock on Søren's fireplace mantel downstairs. It was getting late. He climbed out of bed, started to dress.

"There's no reason to worry," Kingsley said, though he himself was sick with worry. "Closing up a small empire takes time. And Jules loves her doctor here, so I know she won't want to give birth somewhere else. We won't move until the baby's at least six months old." He pulled on his trousers as he talked. Talked, and tried to explain it so clearly that it made so much sense, no one could even think of questioning the decision. "We'll probably even have one last Christmas here before we leave."

"One last Christmas."

"Which is over a year away," Kingsley reminded Søren. And himself. He wasn't leaving tomorrow or the next day. A year, more or less. An entire year. Longer than they had together the first time. It would be enough. It would have to be enough.

"And you're going...where?"

He slid his feet into his boots, a good way to avoid eye contact. "Not certain yet, though I'm thinking a villa in St. Bart's."

"St. Bart's? You mean Saint Barthélemy...the island in the Caribbean." Søren's voice sounded strangely flat.

Kingsley shrugged. "It's French. It's safe. It's close to Haiti. It's beautiful."

"It's 2,000 miles away."

"Only 1,700 miles. I looked it up."

"And that's where Juliette wants to move? St. Bart's?"

"She doesn't know we're moving yet. I'm going to surprise her when we're on holiday in New Orleans."

Søren's eyes widened slightly. "This was *your* idea?"

"What? Do you think Juliette put me up to this? This was my decision. And she'll understand it. I hope you can, too."

The pause before answering was no longer than the space between breaths, but Kingsley felt it like a breath he'd been holding for an hour.

"Of course," Søren said. "If you think for one second that you can't raise your family here safely, then you should go."

"Thank you," Kingsley said. "You know, I didn't make this decision lightly."

"No. Of course you didn't. It's just—"

"What?"

Søren shook his head. "Nothing. St. Bart's is beautiful, I hear. We'll try to visit, if I can."

If.

That word was a bucket of ice water over his head.

If.

Not when.

If.

St. Bart's wasn't a long drive away. St. Bart's wasn't the sort of place one went for a weekend getaway. You could only get there from New

York by flying. Not an easy trip for a small-town priest under a vow of poverty. And if he did come to visit—*if*—where would they go to be alone together? A hotel? It felt tawdry and sad already.

"I'll visit you," Kingsley said.

"Of course."

Another *Of course* and Kingsley would scream. Was that all Søren could say?

"Will you tell Nora or should I?" Kingsley asked.

"No, you can tell her when you're ready to make the announcement. I'd only ask you to wait for a few months. This summer, when it won't hit so hard. Not the holidays."

Was this a punishment, telling Kingsley he had to break the news to Nora himself? *You want to go, you get to tell her the bad news, not me.* Unfair, he knew. It was Kingsley's secret to tell, not Søren's. That's all he meant by that, wasn't it? How terrifyingly fast the doubts were creeping and crawling their way into his brain...

Was Søren already pulling away from him? Shutting him out? De-vesting in their relationship and silently reminding himself, *Now I remember exactly why I chose Nora over you, and why I'll do it again.*

"She'll understand, too," Søren said. "But she will be disappointed. She wanted to be part of the baby's life. She's an only child. No nieces or nephews."

"She can visit anytime. You can, too. I know it's not so easy for you to—"

"We'll be fine."

We'll be fine.

Who was *we*? Was "we" Søren and Kingsley? Søren and Nora? Søren and Kingsley and Nora? All of them? Would they be fine?

An hour ago, he'd felt secure enough to ask Søren the sort of personal questions he wouldn't have dared even think of asking six months ago. Now he couldn't even bring himself to ask who he meant by "we," and who would be "fine" when they were gone.

"I should be going," Kingsley said. "See you soon."

"Of course."

The door waited for him. He'd have to open it and walk through it to go downstairs to leave the house to get into his car to go home. Easy enough, and yet he stood there.

He wanted to kiss Søren goodbye, but he didn't want to risk trying to kiss Søren goodbye and being rejected. Or worse, receiving a tepid kiss. How had a decision that had seemed so simple in theory become so painfully, impossibly difficult?

"If I don't see you before Christmas, I hope you have a nice one," Kingsley said.

A nice one? Was he talking to his lover or a salesgirl at Tiffany's?

"I'm sure it will be fine. You, too. Have a nice time in New Orleans with Juliette."

"We will."

He opened the door. Might as well just do it, like ripping off a bandage. And then he remembered the gauze and tape on his hip and how he had a perfect bloody letter S there that Søren had carved into him, claiming him. He would not let this get between them. He wouldn't. He'd let so many secrets and lies, and his stubborn pride, get between them before. He wasn't a kid anymore, but a grown man with a child on the way. He would not be a coward.

"What were you about to say?" Kingsley asked.

"I didn't say anything," Søren said. He still sat up in the bed, sheets to his hip and his beautiful body suddenly out of reach.

"You started to, a minute ago, and then you stopped yourself. What were you going to say?"

Søren gave a little smile, a cold little smile. "The wrong thing. Trust me."

"I want to hear the wrong thing."

"You don't, I promise—"

"I do. Didn't we just say no more bullshit between us? Didn't we? Or did I imagine that?"

"Kingsley, I know you're—"

"What were you going to say?"

Søren met his eyes. His stare was icy and cold. "I was going to say, 'Don't do this to me again.'"

Kingsley lifted his chin, stood up straighter. "You were right," he said. "That was the wrong thing to say."

"I tried to warn you," Søren said.

"You knew I was in love with you for *years* and you—"

"I know. I know, Kingsley. Of course you have to go. Of course you do."

Kingsley nodded. "Of course."

And with that, he left.

There was no kiss goodnight. Of course there wasn't.

THIRD MOVEMENT

JANUARY MINUET

MINUET:

A slow, stately ballroom dance for two.

CHAPTER TWELVE

JANUARY 5TH and it was seventy degrees at ten in the morning. And, as if it couldn't get any better than that, Kingsley was having some of the better sex of his life, even if it was vanilla.

The window to their rented *pied-à-terre* on Conti Street was open, and a clean morning breeze blew into the bedroom, caressing Kingsley's naked back so lightly that chills rose all over his body. He was on his hands and knees, braced over Juliette, who lay on her back under him, thighs wide and eyes closed, a little smile on her beautifully full, soft lips.

"What are you smiling about?" he demanded, punctuating the question with a gentle thrust. She was so warm inside, warm and slick and so incredibly tight—thank you, pregnancy—that he could have stayed inside her all day.

"Just happy," she said, and slowly opened her eyes. "Very, very happy." *Très, très content.*

Kingsley was also *très, très content.* How could any man in bed with this woman not be *content?*

He felt like he was young and in Paris again, in bed with this glorious woman in their elegantly simple—and simply elegant—apartment on the second floor of an old French Quarter double gallery home. Every morning they were making lazy love on the old creaking brass bed, the pale green shutters thrown open to let in the scent and sounds of city life—coffee, laughing voices, and the thick wet heat of Louisiana.

Juliette was wearing a short cotton nightgown that covered her growing stomach but left her long dark arms and chest bare. He covered her with a thousand soft kisses. Her shoulders, her collarbone, the valley from the hollow of her long throat to between her full breasts. Had they ever had so much vanilla sex in their lives, the two of them? She, who adored being on the receiving end of rough and possessive sex as much as he enjoyed being on the giving end? But there was no risking the baby. Now it was slow. Now it was soft. Now it was lazy and tender, not wicked and rough. Her hands were resting lightly on his shoulders, not tied to the bed. Her legs, hooked over his calves instead of strapped to the footboard, thighs forced open wide.

Eventually, they'd return to their wild nights and wicked ways. For now, Kingsley was more than content to enjoy these sunny, sensual mornings with her. He pulled out and she rolled onto her side, propping her knee up on a pillow. He slid back into her from behind this time, spooning her. While kneading her intensely swollen clitoris, he fucked her. Her breathing quickened, and her head fell back against his shoulder. It was a uniquely satisfying experience to make Juliette—pregnant and dressed in her innocent white cotton maternity nightgown—come so hard he felt her vagina clench around him like the grip of a strong hand, and so loudly, half the French Quarter heard her orgasm. As she was riding the wave of her climax, he pushed into her with ragged breaths and short, shallow thrusts and came hard himself—spending himself until there was nothing left to give her.

Panting and empty, he pulled out and rested his chin against her shoulder. Another soft warm breeze blew through the apartment and rustled the sheer white curtains across the room, making them sway like shy ghosts at a party.

"It's January," she said, laughing like it was a joke. "It's January, and we have the windows open."

"You missed that?" Kingsley asked.

"Warm winters? Oh, yes. This is heaven. You may have to go back to New York without us. We'll see you again in June."

"Coco isn't even here yet, and you two are already ganging up against me."

"Nothing against you," she said. "Only against winter. Ice is not a pregnant woman's best friend. But it's fine. I'll buy some of those spikes climbers put on their boots. What are they called in English? Tampons?"

"Crampons," Kingsley said.

She giggled like a girl. "That's it. Tampons wouldn't do much good on my shoes unless I walked through a puddle." She reached for her phone. It had buzzed while they were making love. "Lord," she said and groaned.

Kingsley took the phone from her. She had a text message from Brad Wolfe—that asshole—asking her out to dinner. "May I?"

"Please," she said.

Kingsley texted a reply.

This is King. Stop asking Juliette out on dates. She is pregnant with my baby.

He thought that would do it. Brad Wolfe—that asshole—wrote back immediately.

The more, the merrier.

Asshole, Kingsley replied, then blocked Wolfe's number before returning Juliette's phone to her.

"Not to blame the victim," he said, "but it's your fault you're so beautiful."

"It's a curse, I know." She laughed again, and he pulled her closer and gently cradled her belly.

"You think we woke Coco up?"

"I felt a little wiggling in there." Juliette placed her hand over his and moved it. "There. Feel it?"

He did feel it, the little hand or foot pushing against the walls of the womb. Sometimes Juliette would balance a small cup of water on her belly and wait for the water to dance in the glass. She would say, *Oh, no, the T-Rex is coming...*

"Does it hurt?" he asked.

"Not really. Coco is a good roommate. Lots more dancing since we came here, though. I think Coco likes the French Quarter."

"Coco likes all the beignets you've been eating."

Juliette gasped dramatically. "Beignets? What a wonderful idea..." She rolled over to face him, a maneuver she liked to call a walrus pirouette. "That's exactly what we should have after breakfast."

"After breakfast? What are we having *for* breakfast?"

"Blueberry waffles, coush-coush, and omelets."

"That's it?"

She poked him in the center of his chest. "Extra powdered sugar on the beignets, remember."

"Yes, ma'am."

He dressed quickly. Before leaving, he paused in the kitchen doorway and watched Juliette cook. She was singing *"Parlez-Moi d'Amour"* to herself as she sliced onions and mushrooms, massaged olive oil into the flesh of bright red bell peppers. She'd bought a New Orleans-themed cookbook on their second day here, and every morning she tried a new recipe. In the two weeks they'd been here, Juliette had bloomed like a rose. He hadn't realized how much the cold of Manhattan's bitter winters bothered her until he watched her come alive under the January sun of New Orleans.

"I have a present for you," he said.

She glanced at him, gave him that sly smile he always loved to see. "Another one?"

"I saved the best for last. I'll give it to you after breakfast."

"We're taking the streetcar tour after breakfast."

"I'll give it to you on the streetcar."

"Ah, then it's not what I thought it was."

"Maybe it is," he said, "and I just want us to get kicked off the streetcar." He kissed her soft cheek. "I'll be back with beignets. Extra powdered sugar. Decaf coffee for you."

"Kink and caffeine—the only two things I miss from BC." *Before Coco.*

"I promise, after the baby's here and you're ready, we'll drink espresso and have kinky sex all night."

"That's all I ask," she said.

Kingsley turned to leave, and she gave him a playful pinch on his French derriere on his way out of the kitchen. Really, she was a changed woman here. Relaxed, giggly, walls down, as if the city had gotten her drunk. He was falling in love with her all over again. The first time he fell for her, it was for her sorrow. Now he found himself falling even harder for her joy.

If this is what life would be like when they moved to St. Bart's, then he was ready to pack up today and leave the empire dismantling to the lawyers. Only, he knew it didn't work that way. And even if it did, he'd promised Søren one last Christmas. How could he take that back? Especially since he hadn't made that promise for Søren's sake, but for his own.

He strolled along the breezy sunlit streets of

the Old Square, sunglasses on, which made it easier to note the appreciative glances he received from the female tourists that morning. Every sundress that walked past him did a double-take or, even bolder, shot him a smile. He was wearing his favorite jeans with a loose white button-down shirt half-tucked in, collar open, sleeves rolled up. He knew he looked like he'd just rolled out of the bed of a beautiful woman—which was accurate. When he passed the hostess at a French café, she smiled broadly at him. "*Bonjour,*" he said, forgetting to switch to English. He and Juliette always spoke French when alone together.

The waitress replied, *"Bonjour, Monsieur. Voulez-vous vous joindre à nous pour le petit déjeuner?"*

"Not today," he replied—*Pas aujourd-hui*—hoping his look of surprise was hidden behind his sunglasses. "Maybe tomorrow."

She smiled broadly. A sure sign she was American, not French.

"Your French is very good," he said to her. She looked about twenty, a young Black college girl wearing the classic hostess uniform of a black skirt with a white blouse. "You've been to France?"

"Not yet. I graduated from the *Ecole Bilingue* last year," she said.

"It's a French school? Here?" He hadn't realized they had French immersion schools in New Orleans. He assumed it was as French as Boston was Irish—in symbol and spirit, but not really.

She nodded. "There are a few in town. They're trying to bring the language back."

"You had good teachers. And I'm from Paris, so only my opinion counts."

She smiled again and made him promise to come for breakfast tomorrow with his girlfriend. A pinky swear was demanded and given. As Kingsley walked off toward Café du Monde, he caught himself feeling that same happiness he'd felt the night of his birthday. Only here, now, the fear was gone. Had he left it in Manhattan or lost it in New Orleans? Either way, *laissez le bon temps rouler...*

CHAPTER THIRTEEN

AT NOON THEY BOARDED A STREETCAR—NOT named *Desire*, sadly—for a tour of the Garden District. Kingsley had been to New Orleans before. Mardi Gras, years ago. His memory of the city was only of its nightlife. He had stayed out until dawn, returned to his hotel, and slept all day before going out again in the evening. Other than the parties and the parade, he hadn't seen much of the city. He certainly hadn't done any daylight tourist activities. Not his style. But Juliette loved looking at old houses—she had a Gothic streak in her bones a mile wide—and what made her happy made him happy.

Shamelessly, Juliette took photo after photo with her phone, like every other tourist on the streetcar. When the tour guide, speaking in an almost-impenetrable Cajun accent, pointed out Anne Rice's old house, Juliette took a dozen photos of it and immediately texted them to Nora.

"She would love it here," Juliette said.

Kingsley had to agree. Mistress Nora would do well in a city known as The Big Easy. Art. Literature. Sin. Booze. What more could a porno-writing Catholic dominatrix want? Maybe they would come back next autumn, all of them together for one last hurrah before he and Juliette decamped to St. Bart's.

"Are you sure we have to leave Sunday?" Juliette asked as they turned a corner, and the streetcar eased slowly down a street so dense with ancient oaks that they blocked the sun.

"We could try to get a hotel and stay another week, if you like."

"You probably have too much to do back home."

"If you want to stay, we'll stay," he said.

She smiled, almost wistfully, and put her hand over her belly. "We have a doctor's appointment on Tuesday. I shouldn't miss it."

"We can come back after." He put his arm around her shoulders. She nestled in closer to him...for about two seconds, before she decided she needed to hang out the side of the streetcar to take more photos. "I know you're not looking forward to another winter in New York."

"Who would be?" she said without turning.

"What would you say if I told you we only had to stay there one more winter?"

Slowly, she lowered her phone and ducked back into the streetcar, a dozen beautiful old houses sliding by unseen, forgotten.

"What do you mean?" she asked.

"I mean...I want us to move away, start over somewhere safer. Warmer."

They had taken their seats near the back so they could speak without interrupting the other tourists. He was glad now that they had a little privacy. Juliette covered her mouth with her hand and glanced away.

"It'll be for the best," he said. "I was thinking St. Bart's. Safe, beautiful. Our children will grow up speaking French. We'll get a villa there. No more winters."

She turned around and looked at him. "You can't mean it." She lowered her voice and added, "What about Søren?"

"He knows."

Her lovely dark eyes widened. "You already told him?"

"I already told him," he said. "A few weeks ago. It's done. Call it a *fait accompli.*"

Because it was a *fait accompli* if he'd already told Søren. Because that was the hardest part, the biggest barrier, the only thing standing in their way. Nothing could stop them now.

"But the clubs—"

"We'll sell them. Or I'll find someone to take over The 8th Circle."

"Who would run it?"

"The King is retired. Long live the Queen?"

Juliette nodded. "Nora would do an excellent job. But the townhouse—"

"We'll sell it. We could buy ten of these," he said, pointing at a row of ivy-draped Louisiana mansions, "for the price of one Manhattan townhouse on Riverside Drive."

Juliette shook her head—not to say no, but because she was clearly in shock and couldn't quite take it all in yet. They rode the next few blocks in silence, not even hearing what their tour guide had to say about the cemetery, about the beads on the trees and fences...

"I never let myself dream," she said, and looked at him again. "But you already told him."

He nodded slowly.

Again, she shook her head. "I thought you'd never give up the city and the clubs and the power...then I thought you might, after all that happened. But then you and he—and you were so happy, and I was happy for you, but I told myself now it would never happen. And that was fine. New York is fine. It's only..."

"It's not where you want to be. And if you don't want to be there, I don't want to be there."

She rested against his chest again, her hand on his heart, and his chin on the top of her head.

"You were right," she said. "This is the best gift."

He kissed her hair. "You're missing a good house," he whispered.

She sat back up and turned with her phone to take a picture of an enormous white mansion with a black iron fence surrounding it, a large yard filled with tropical plants and an imposing portico with four white columns. It was the sort of house children dream of living one day. A true dream house. Even now, Kingsley was daydreaming of their children playing hide-and-seek in a garden like that, playing fetch with a dog in a yard like that, growing up safe and coddled and spoiled and loved in a house like that.

"If anyone has a spare eight million on them," the tour guide said, "that one's for sale. It's a fixer-upper."

Juliette laughed and looked at him. "How much do you have in your wallet?"

❄

AFTER THE STREETCAR TOUR, they went out in search of lunch. Juliette joked she was on the hobbit diet now that she was pregnant: first breakfast, second breakfast, elevenses, lunch, dinner, tea, supper. Kingsley was happy to indulge her. New Orleans had surprised him with the incredible variety and quality of their restaurants. The whole city was putting Manhattan to shame.

As they strolled toward the cafe, hand in hand, Juliette said, "You know, St. Bart's is tiny. I mean...*teeny* tiny. I checked my phone. The whole population is less than ten thousand people. Could you survive living in a small town on an island?"

"For you I could."

"Have you ever lived on an island for longer than a month or two? It's harder than people think. Especially if you're not used to it. I was used to it, and even I got island fever."

"It doesn't have to be St. Bart's. I only

thought of it because it was French and safe and one flight to see your mother. We could move to L.A. if you wanted, San Diego, Miami—"

Suddenly she stopped and gave a little laugh. "Look," she said, pointing.

Across the street came a row of children, girls, all of them about nine or ten years old. They were wearing matching dresses, gray plaid with crisp white shirts and black cardigans. A young nun in a gray habit led them, a goose and her goslings.

"Aww..." Juliette sighed and leaned against him. "They look just like Madeline."

"Who?"

"The little French girl in the children's books?" Juliette said as if he should know that. She recited a few lines for him:

In an old house in Paris
That was covered with vines
Lived twelve little girls
In two straight lines [...]
The smallest one was Madeline.

"Boys didn't read Madeline books," he said.

"I wanted to be her so badly," Juliette said, shaking her head. "I had all the books and read them over and over. I remember getting in trouble for trying to color Madeline in with a brown crayon so she'd look more like me. But those girls, they look just like the girls in the books, except they *do* look like me."

The girls in the Catholic-school uniforms

were Black like Juliette. Even the nun was Black. Juliette raised her hand and waved at the girls as they passed. They waved back, smiling broadly.

"Are you having a baby?" one girl shouted across the street.

"Yes, we are," Juliette called back. "Soon!"

Some of the girls applauded and a couple *oooh*-ed, which prompted the nun to turn and shush them. Kingsley laughed. This was not something that happened in Manhattan. If you waved at strangers across the street and talked with them, people would think you were mentally unstable. It seemed so natural here. So easy.

Ah, The Big Easy. So that's how it got its name.

Juliette laughed, too, but her eyes were filled with tears, ready to spill.

"Jules?"

The girls turned the corner and disappeared. Juliette stared at where they had been and where they went as if she saw something he couldn't see.

"I never told you," she said, "but I've been here before."

More secrets.

"I thought this was your first trip," Kingsley said. Was everyone in his life keeping secrets from him?

"He brought me here, once. Only once."

He. The man who'd practically kept her a prisoner, blackmailing her into obedience. Juliette hardly ever spoke of him but when she did, she never said his name, only "he" or "him."

"I ran away from him here," she said. "I was on my own for two days. When I remembered he was paying for my mother's treatment, I went back. The two best days of my life were in this city." She smiled. "Until you."

He held out his hand to her and she took it, squeezed it, met his eyes. "Let's move here," she said.

"New Orleans."

"Why not? It's French. It's a big city, a real city. Far, far from New York. And Coco would grow up with children that looked like her, or him. And the music and the food..."

He held up his hand. "If this is what you want—"

"It's what I want."

"It's settled then," he said. "We'll start looking for houses."

"Good. But lunch first, please."

They sat at a table outside on the café's patio. Eating outside in January? Maybe August would be hell, but it would be worth going through it for this—Juliette in a bright yellow sundress and sandals in the middle of winter, happier than he'd seen her since the day she first felt the baby kick, when the theoretical had become so wonderfully real.

While Juliette was in the bathroom, Kingsley sent Søren a message.

We're still moving, but it's New Orleans, not St. Bart's.

Without waiting for a reply, he added, *I miss you,* and immediately he wished he hadn't.

Juliette returned, and he helped her into her chair. As she perused the specials, she suddenly looked up. She smiled, then hid her face behind the menu.

"What? What is it?" Kingsley asked.

"Don't look behind you," she whispered.

He immediately looked behind him. Two priests in black clerical garb and Roman collars —a white priest, white-haired, about sixty, and a young Korean priest, not more than thirty— took a table at the opposite end of the patio. Before they could say anything, their waitress came to the table with their coffee.

"Morning, Katie," the younger priest said with a wave to their waitress.

"Morning, Father Lee." She smiled at Kingsley and Juliette. "Cream and sugar?"

"Please," Juliette said. "And do you know those priests?'

"They're in all the time. Jesuits from the college. They get free coffee here."

The waitress walked over to the priests and joined them in friendly conversation.

"You think it's a sign?" Juliette said.

"Definitely," Kingsley said. "I'll just trade in my Jesuit for a new one."

Juliette reached across the table and took his hand in hers. "Thank you, my love," she said softly. *Merci, mon amour.* "We'll find a way to make this work. For all of us."

"Are you happy?"

"Very."

"Then it's already working," he said,

squeezing her hand. “Merry Christmas, my jewel.”

“Merry Christmas, *mon roi.*”

As Kingsley went to put his phone away—he considered texting during a meal to be a mortal sin—it buzzed in his hand. A cryptic reply from Søren.

Much better.

FOURTH MOVEMENT

FEBRUARY SONATA

SONATA:

An instrumental musical composition typically of three or four movements in contrasting forms and keys.

CHAPTER FOURTEEN

KINGSLEY GAZED into the pit below him. Quiet this Monday evening, far quieter than the madness of a Friday or Saturday. Not empty, however. A dominant man wearing only leather trousers and full sleeve tattoos worked his submissive girlfriend over with a flogger on a St. Andrew's Cross. One of the "littles" who belonged to a man called Papa Bear was swinging upside-down from a harness, her frilly panties on full display as her dress hung over her head. Otherwise, fairly subdued down there.

At least the dungeons were full. All four of his staff dominatrixes were hard at work, putting the fear of Goddess into their wealthy male clients. It was good, he reminded himself, that these people—his people—had a safe place to play. The equipment was of high quality. The pro dommes and subs were world-class. And when the party got going, it was like Hieronymus Bosch's wettest dream.

There had been a time when wild horses

couldn't drag him out of the club. Now it was hardly ten at night, and already he was checking his watch, longing to be home with Juliette. They could read each other books about New Orleans, discuss renovations, paint colors, nannies... He tried to tell himself The Big Easy wasn't all jazz and booze, beignets and Mardi Gras. There was something called "termite season," apparently. And God, the lizards—they were *everywhere*. Devastating poverty in many of the wards, not to mention the rampant post-Katrina gentrification. And, of course, the summer humidity you could cut with a chainsaw. He reminded himself of all these downsides, but it didn't work. He still wanted to be there more than he wanted to be in this city.

The future tantalized him. The past dogged him. When he wasn't imagining life in New Orleans with Juliette and their baby, he was back in the past again, sixteen years old, following Søren one warm September night out to a clearing in the Maine woods, waiting to hear those three words again—

"There's my King," came a voice from behind him.

Wrong three words.

Mistress Nora put her hands on his hips from behind and rose up to kiss his cheek. He leaned into the kiss. She sidled up next to him at the railing. She was wearing a red leather bustier and red boots. A short flogger with scarlet tails hung from a cord around her wrist. "Watching the show?"

"Not much of one tonight. It's Monday," he said with a shrug.

She swept her thick black hair off her shoulders and pulled it up into a loose bun, then fanned herself. Must have just finished up with a client. Her hair was damp with sweat, and her heavy black eye make-up was becomingly smudged. Her dark eyes glowed bright by the light of the tall tallow candles that illuminated the VIP lounge. For a moment, he could imagine she was a Valkyrie, fierce, deadly, and wild.

"How was your session?" he asked. He wanted desperately to tell her what he and Juliette were planning, but Søren had asked him to wait for a few months so she could get her bearings. They'd been through a lot, especially her.

"It was all right. I think I broke his finger. Oops."

Oops? Not merely sadistic, but callous, too. Kingsley's blood stirred just standing next to her, and he wondered if he needed a beating tonight more than he needed his dignity. No, he told himself, not tonight. Tonight he would go home as soon as he could, get out of his clothes—obscenely snug black trousers, black shirt with the collar open, and black coat with tails—and into bed with Juliette.

"Is that bad?" he asked.

"Nah. He tips an extra grand if I break something."

"You don't sound excited."

She glanced at him out the corner of her eye. "Can I tell you a secret without you firing me?"

"You don't work for me anymore, remember?"

Painfully, this was true. Nora chose her own clients now. She kept all her money. She paid rent on her dungeon, but she didn't answer to him anymore. This arrangement had hurt his wallet but improved their relationship.

"Okay, fine," she said. "Can I tell you a secret without you kicking me out of my dungeon?"

"Of course."

"I broke his finger because I was bored, and I was trying to do something to get my head back in the game."

"I take it this didn't work."

"Worked for him." She rolled her eyes. "He came so hard I have to get the ceilings mopped tomorrow. Still, the whole time I was thinking about how I wanted to be anywhere in the world but in that room."

"You never think that when I'm in your dungeon, do you?"

She put her arm around his waist, patted his ass, and kissed his cheek. His tight trousers were getting even tighter. This woman was so vicious that breaking a man's finger bored her.

"Never," she said with a wicked gleam in her vicious eyes. "When I'm with you—dungeon or no dungeon—all I can think about is how much fun I have beating the shit out of you."

"*Merci.*"

He kissed her lips lightly, and they turned

their gazes back to the pit. A few more people had trickled in. Play was picking up. Someone was getting their boots blacked. Someone else was getting pilloried and sodomized in tandem.

"I was torturing a billionaire, and I was bored," she said.

"And I'm watching a former child star get sodomized by a drag queen named Scarlet O'Whora, and I'm bored, too. What's wrong with us?"

"It's that room," she said, sober again, somber. He knew she wasn't talking about her dungeon this time. She wrapped her arms around herself as if suddenly cold. "Something happened in that room to us, and we're all different now. You feel it, don't you?"

"I feel it."

"Looking back, it feels like I spent my entire adult life playing with people."

"You did. That was your job."

"True." She sighed. "For years it was like the three of us were playing one big game with each other. Me and him versus you. You and him versus me. Me and you versus him. I don't know. It's like...after everything that happened, the game's over."

"Because we both won?" Kingsley asked.

She met his eyes. "Because maybe it was never a game to start with." She closed her eyes. "So many people got hurt. We hurt so many people. Real pain is a lot scarier than what they pay me for."

"Yes," he said. "Yes, it is."

"It's hard to be here sometimes," she said. "I keep trying to go back to the way things were, but I don't know... I'm starting to think I'm not supposed to go back. I'm supposed to go forward."

Had she told Søren that? Is that why he didn't want Kingsley to tell her they were moving, because she was feeling just as restless? If Kingsley and Juliette left, if they broke the bond that held them all together, what would stop Nora from leaving, too? Her black eyes glowed with an inner fire. No wonder Søren feared getting burned again.

Intrigued but unwilling to show his hand, Kingsley said simply, "Where do you think you are supposed to go?"

"I want to travel. Get out of here and not look back for a while. In fact, I was thinking..." She glanced at him out the corner of her eye. "You told me a long time ago about this place you went to in France after you got shot the first time. Somewhere in wine country or something. Your parents took you there when you were a kid?"

Kingsley furrowed his brow. "I told you about that? I don't remember."

She smiled. "You were drunk at the time. I think I was, too. You said you went somewhere to recuperate? Maybe that's what I need. A little time in wine country."

What she needed was a male submissive. A real one. Not her old houseboy Wesley or whatever his stupid name was, but a real submissive who would worship her for her power, not try to take it away from her. Someone to serve her, guard her, someone she could train and spoil and be spoiled by. Not that he would tell her that and risk being bludgeoned to death by Søren. Bludgeoning was one of his few hard limits.

He waved his hand to dismiss the idea. "You'll be bored," he said. "Just a little village called Mozet and a bit of beach. My father had friends there, I think. It's been so long since I've been."

"Didn't you have a girlfriend there?"

"No, I had a *wife* there. Only she was someone else's wife."

Nora laughed her low throaty laugh, and he had to remind himself—again—that he was going to go home as soon as possible. Any minute now.

"Mozet," she said as if committing the name to memory. "I'll look it up. Maybe it's just what the doctor ordered."

"Juliette had a good time in New Orleans, you know. You could take a few weeks there. We didn't want to come back."

"So I heard. Søren asked me if I'd seen you since you got back from your trip. You aren't hiding from him, are you?"

Kingsley exhaled heavily. "Maybe. I think I've gotten on his bad side again."

"What did you do?" Her tone was teasing.

"I told him something he didn't want to hear."

"That'll do it. But I don't think he's mad at you at all."

"Are you sure?"

"He's been playing Vivaldi's 'Winter' over and over again like some kind of Phantom of the Rectory. It's very adorable, not that I told him that. I think he's pining for you. I know he's not pining for me. He can't get rid of me."

Kingsley tried not to smile, though it was hard. Kingsley thought he was the one who did all the pining in their relationship.

"Perhaps he's just in the mood to play Vivaldi," he said.

Kingsley had written a report on Vivaldi back at their old school. Vivaldi, the "Red Priest" who taught music to orphan girls, turning many of them into violin virtuosos.

"He also just bought you another Christmas present," Nora said. "It's sitting on his piano with your name on it."

"He did? What is it?"

"No clue. He's being secretive about it. Then again, I'm being secretive, too." She brought the tips of her fingers together and wiggled them rapidly, like a mad scientist fiendishly delighted by the potion she was brewing.

He leaned close to her. "What secret are you keeping?" he whispered.

"If I tell you," she said, "it won't be a secret."

A soft buzzing interrupted them, a phone vibrating. Nora took her phone out of her bustier where she'd nestled it between her ample breasts. Lucky phone.

"I better go," she said. "I'm spanking the mayor's nephew in ten. This one I'm actually looking forward to. He's cute as a button when you put him in stockings, garters, and a Laura Ashley dress."

She kissed Kingsley on the cheek, but before she could pull away, he took her by the wrist. "Before you go, I was thinking..."

She waited, eyes wide, and he saw the real woman underneath the outrageous make-up—the blood-red lips and Cleopatra eyes. Nora. His friend. One of the very few people he trusted with his life.

"When the baby comes, I was going to take some time off to help Juliette," he said. "But someone has to watch over the clubs, you know. I was wondering—"

"Not me."

That surprised him. He thought she'd jump at the chance to rule his empire. "Not you?"

"I... This is going to sound embarrassing and entirely out of character, so please just forget I've said it after I've said it. Okay?"

"Okay..."

"Most nights, all I want is to be with Søren," she said. "Not even for sex or kink. Just with him. It's a good thing I've scared him off asking me to marry him. If he asked me to elope to San Pedro tomorrow, I might do it."

She was serious.

"And if you tell him that," she added, "I will kill you."

She was serious about that, too.

"Is it that bad?" he asked.

"Or good? I don't know. I just know I've turned down twenty clients this past month. I'm down to ten sessions a week. My therapist says that's normal, that it takes six months at least to get your bearings back after a life-altering incident. Unfortunately, the bills don't wait for you to get your shit together."

Søren had said Nora was struggling, that she was "fragile." And perhaps she was. But she wasn't fragile like a wine glass, Kingsley saw, but fragile like an egg. There was something inside her about to break out. No wonder Søren was scared. Was he scared *for* her or *of* her?

"You know I will help you if you need it," Kingsley said.

"If it comes to begging you for money, I'll start stealing cars again." Her phone buzzed. "I better run. Places to go. People to beat."

Her old joke, except this time she didn't smile when she said it. She kissed him one more time and turned to walk away.

Then she stopped and spun on her heel, turning like a music box ballerina. It was good to see that even if she'd lost her bloodlust, she hadn't lost her grace.

"I know who could run the place while you're on paternity leave."

CHAPTER FIFTEEN

IT TOOK a second for Kingsley to recognize the young man who answered the door. Shaggy dark hair, wide silver-blue eyes that somehow managed to look both innocent and intelligent at the same time. He wore baggy khakis on his thin frame and a navy-blue t-shirt with YORKE written across the front. Yorke College.

"Michael," Kingsley said. "You cut your hair."

"Ah, yeah," he said and ran a hand over his head as if still getting used to his shorter hair. "For Christmas. I was trying to look older since we were visiting Griff's family. Did it work?"

"You do look older. But why aren't you at school?" It was a Tuesday evening, and not a holiday as far as Kingsley knew.

"The furnace in my dorm died. The temperature dropped to forty indoors, so they sent us all home. Or, not home, you know, but—"

"Here."

Michael blushed becomingly. He really was a

pretty boy. No wonder Griffin had fallen so hard for him so fast.

"If that's our Mexican," Griffin's voice carried all the way from down the hall, "the money's on the side table."

"I'm French, not Mexican," Kingsley called back before Michael could reply.

Griffin suddenly stuck his head into the short hallway of their apartment. "King, holy fuck."

Griffin ran to the door and slid the last few yards on his socks, coming to a stop only by grabbing the door frame. Kingsley took a self-preserving step back just in case.

"King."

"Griffin."

"I swear to God, we're getting Mexican food for dinner. We weren't planning a racist threesome."

"I assumed."

"God, I haven't seen you in forever, man. Get in here. Hug me 'til it hurts."

Kingsley sighed. Griffin was...Griffin. As usual. The hug was brief but painful, just the way Griffin liked it.

Before Kingsley knew it, he was sitting in a black club chair with a cup of a very good coffee in his hand. Griffin took a seat on the sofa, with Michael at his feet, shoulders between his knees. Outside, fresh snow was falling, and the sky had turned a strange smoky gray. The apartment was warm but not quite Kingsley's style. Exposed brick walls. Sleek, symmetrical black leather furniture. Funky cow-print rugs. A playful home, but definitely on the young side. Or maybe Kingsley was just getting to be on the old side.

Griffin grilled him about his "babymoon" while Michael listened quietly and politely, only occasionally offering his own questions or comments. Every time Michael did speak up, Griffin would gently squeeze his shoulder or tug his hair as if to reward him for talking. He was a shy kid, Kingsley knew, and Griffin seemed to be helping him out of his shell. He did have a way of making people comfortable, making them feel safe to be themselves. This would stand him in good stead if he took the job Kingsley came to offer.

"Since your dinner is on the way, I'll get to the point," Kingsley said as he set his empty mug on the rustic wood coffee table. Wood. Splinters. Sharp square corners. Not child-safe at all.

"Or just stay for dinner," Griffin offered. "We always order extra. Trying to fatten Mick up so we can share clothes."

"It's not working," Michael said. "So much for the freshman fifteen."

"I'll give you fifteen lashes later tonight," Griffin said. "That can be your freshman fifteen."

"You know we have a guest, right?" Michael pointed to Kingsley. "Like...right there. And he can hear you."

"King," Griffin said, "I'm going to give Mick fifteen lashes later tonight."

"As you should. He clearly hasn't learned his place yet." Kingsley winked at Michael.

"I'm just kidding. Mick knows he's perfect." Griffin leaned over and gave Michael a quick rough hug and a kiss. They were so easy together, so comfortable. Would Kingsley ever be that comfortable, that playful with Søren? He'd known and loved the man since he was sixteen years old, and he still couldn't imagine coming up behind Søren and giving him a hug. He'd probably end up in the hospital after taking an elbow to the liver.

"All right, so I'm curious now," Griffin said. "What's up?"

"First, I have to ask you to keep this a secret. For now. Just for now."

"From who? Everyone? Like, even Nora?"

"Yes."

"Should I go?" Michael looked up at Griffin. "I can go."

"Whatever he tells me, I'll tell you anyway," Griffin said. "King knows that."

"Yes, I know that." Ah, to be that young and naïve again.

Griffin and Michael listened intently as Kingsley explained the situation to them—Juliette's pregnancy, feeling unsafe in the city after what they'd all gone through, the enemies he'd made, and the decision he'd come to...and, of course, the need for someone to watch over The 8th Circle and its denizens.

"Mistress Nora herself suggested you,"

Kingsley said. "And I'm inclined to agree with her opinion."

Griffin looked incredulous. "Me? Seriously? Run The 8th Circle?"

"You. Seriously."

"That's a...that's huge, King. Are you really leaving? I can't imagine New York without you, or I guess...you without New York."

"I can imagine it very easily. And maybe when you're my age, you can imagine it, too."

"And this is like...a done deal?"

"We found a house," Kingsley said. "It's old, however, and in a city that's hard on houses. We're looking at a massive renovation that would take about a year. As I told Søren, we'll have one last Christmas here and then move next January, February at the latest. That's not much time to train a replacement to run an empire."

"So...you need an answer pretty fast."

Kingsley nodded. "I won't be angry if you say no. It's not easy."

Griffin shrugged. "Fuck, what else do I have to do besides keep him in line two days a week?" He tugged Michael's hair.

"Is that a yes?"

"Let me talk to Mick about it. I'll tell you in a week or two?"

Kingsley smiled. "*Parfait.*"

Griffin met his eyes and looked suddenly very serious. It wasn't often one witnessed Griffin Fiske being serious. "What happens if I say no? You have a runner-up?"

"You don't need to worry about that."

"Why? Because it'll influence my decision?"

"You'll sell it," Michael said.

Kingsley glanced down at Michael's uncanny silver eyes, but didn't say anything. That told them everything.

"Shit," Griffin said, falling back onto the couch. "So it's me or the club folds."

"There are other clubs in town."

"There's no other 8th Circle."

"And there are very few people I trust," Kingsley said. "Nora said she's in no shape yet to take on the responsibility. She would trust you to do it, and so would I. But no one else."

Griffin blew out a hard breath. "All right. Let me think about it."

"It does make good money. Not that you need it, but it's been lucrative."

"Wouldn't kill me to have a real job for once in my life."

Kingsley agreed, but he didn't say so out loud. He knew far too many depressed and anxious trust-fund babies whose lives drifted along listlessly, without purpose or meaning.

The door buzzer sounded.

"I should go," Kingsley said. "I believe your Mexican has arrived."

He was on his way to the elevator when Griffin caught up with him. "Hey, King, wait up."

Kingsley turned and saw Griffin wearing that same uncharacteristically serious expression on his handsome face. His dark eyes were shadowed. His lips were tight.

"How's Nora doing?" Griffin asked. "Seriously."

Kingsley mulled that question over before answering. "I don't know. Søren says she's struggling. I saw her just last night, and she admitted to feeling not quite herself. None of us do, I think."

"Is that why you're not telling her you're moving?"

"Søren's asked me to wait while she gets her bearings."

"You know she'll be pissed when she finds out we're keeping something from her."

"There are two possible outcomes," Kingsley said. "One, she'll understand and appreciate that we were only trying to help her. Or two...she'll beat the shit out of me and Søren."

"Hey, win-win."

"And you."

"Not a win. Definitely not a win."

The ancient elevator door opened.

"Goodnight, Griffin."

"Hey, speaking of the sinister minister..." He lifted his chin. "What's going on with you and Søren?"

Kingsley only smiled and hit the CLOSE DOOR button. "I said, *Goodnight, Griffin.*"

❄

No Rolls Royce was awaiting Kingsley at the curb. He'd been traveling incognito since coming home from New Orleans, and caught a cab. He was planning to head straight home until he saw the glow of Central Park and asked to be let out there.

He buttoned his wool coat and walked with his hands in his pockets, enjoying the pleasant crunch of fresh snow under his shoes as he strolled on the snow-packed lanes. The park was straight out of an old postcard tonight. It was only one of the many things he loved about New York.

What was it Nora told him once about leaving Søren? That there are two reasons you leave someone you're still in love with: either it's the right thing to do, or it's the only thing to do. With her and Søren, leaving him had been the only way for her to live the life she needed to live. With Kingsley and Manhattan...ah, it wasn't the only thing to do, no, but leaving was the right thing to do. For Juliette. For Coco. For himself. He only hoped that someday Søren would understand Kingsley wasn't leaving him again, just the city that could no longer keep them safe.

Don't do this to me again.

Those words echoed in his mind. Søren had warned him it was the wrong thing to say. And it had been. That night.

But tonight? Tonight, Kingsley found himself smiling at the memory of those words, the heartfelt pain behind them. Kingsley had left

Søren. That was a fact. He'd left, disappeared, not come back. And all the while, he later learned, Søren had been waiting for him, wanting him, even searching for him with a Paris Saint-Germain football shirt in his old schoolbag wrapped in brown paper and tied with twine.

That wasn't something a man without a heart would do.

That was something a man with a broken heart would do.

And what if Kingsley was breaking his heart again by keeping his distance? Only one way to find out.

It was embarrassing how much mental effort it took for Kingsley to call Søren.

As soon as Søren answered, Kingsley said, "What did you get me for Christmas?"

A soft mocking laugh. "Who told you I got you anything?"

"Nora."

"She'll be flogged for that. I was saving your present for our last Christmas together."

"You mean in ten months?" Kingsley said.

"Yes."

"You were going to keep a present out in plain sight for ten months? That's torture."

"Of course it is. The torture is half the gift."

Kingsley grinned and leaned back against a lamppost. "Can't we consider it a late Christmas gift from last year?"

"We can. But only if you come over tonight to open it."

A yellow cab moved slowly down the street toward him. Kingsley raised his arm.

"I'm on my way. I need to stop by the house first and pick up your souvenir from New Orleans."

"Why am I suddenly terrified?"

"Because you should be," Kingsley said. "See you soon."

"I miss you, too."

The cab pulled to the curb. Kingsley was frozen to the spot, though, phone to his ear. He couldn't believe what he'd heard. "What was that?"

"You texted me from New Orleans and said you miss me," Søren said. "And I said, *I miss you, too*."

Kingsley nearly laughed. "You really do love me, then."

"I do. Are you finally getting used to that?"

Kingsley breathed out a thick exhale that hung in the air.

"Almost."

CHAPTER SIXTEEN

When Kingsley arrived at the rectory, he heard music wafting through the door. He stopped before entering, listened. Was that Vivaldi's "Winter" from *Four Seasons*? He quietly opened the door.

He passed through the cozy old kitchen with its hardwood floors worn slick by time and stood in the arched entryway to the living room. The fire was bright in the fireplace and Søren sat with his back to Kingsley at the piano, still playing as if he hadn't heard Kingsley come into the house.

Kingsley told himself he shouldn't do it...but he also told himself he wanted to do it. He'd envied Griffin and Michael their easy way with each other. Yet he knew that would never be him and Søren. His lover didn't like being touched when he wasn't ready for it. And knowing that, respecting that, was a deeper, more meaningful type of intimacy than just walking up behind your lover and embracing them. So Kingsley waited until the piece came to an end.

Søren's fingers lifted off the keys, and he rested his hands on his lap.

Kingsley approached, with loud footfalls. Søren didn't face him until Kingsley was setting his gift on the piano.

Søren picked up the black bag. The cuffs of his black, long-sleeved pullover were pushed up to reveal his forearms. For some reason, Søren also liked to play piano in bare feet. Something about feeling the vibrations of the music through the floor.

"What's in the bag?" Søren asked.

"Just a souvenir from New Orleans."

"If it's not beignets, I'm going to be a little disappointed," Søren said.

"It's not beignets. I can't have those in the house without eating a dozen of them."

Søren pulled the tissue from the bag, revealing a mask in the old Venetian style. It was painted red on one side, solid white on the other, with elaborate gilding around the mouth and eyes. The work of a famous local artist, popular at Mardi Gras.

Søren examined the mask closely. "This is disturbing. I assume that's the point?"

"It might be."

Søren put on the mask and was transformed into a strange and mysterious blank-faced figure, a nightmare come to life.

"Take it off," Kingsley said. "It's too bizarre. This was a mistake. Huge mistake."

Søren didn't take it off. He just laughed a low sinister laugh. Nora was right. He was the fucking Phantom of the Rectory.

"Just toss it in the trash," Kingsley said.

"Oh no. I'll find a use for it." He set the mask on the top of the piano, where it looked like a face was trying to escape a pool of liquid ebony. "Thank you. It's good to see you again."

"Nora said you were pining for me."

"I do not pine. But," Søren said, his tone conciliatory, "you have been on my mind."

"She said you were playing 'Winter' in my honor. Why that piece?" Kingsley asked. "Vivaldi wasn't French."

"When I was twenty, living in Rome at school, I went to Magdalena's house for Christmas. I'd said something to her months earlier about you, how I was worried you might be dead. After losing your parents and your sister, it wasn't out of the realm of possibility that you'd commit suicide or drink yourself to death. That night, Magda had me play that song for her on her new piano. As she was turning the pages of the sheet music, suddenly....there you were."

"There I was?"

"A picture of you. She'd hired an investigator to find you."

Kingsley stared, wide-eyed. "You knew where I was?"

Søren shook his head. "Magda was too much of a sadist to tell me. She showed me you were alive, as I'd wished, and nothing else. Besides, I was already in the Jesuits by then, and I knew if you wanted me, you could have found me. All you had to do was—"

"Call our school. I did."

Now it was Søren's turn to be struck silent.

"I called a couple of times but never could bring myself to leave a message for you," Kingsley said. "Too much of a coward to face you. I didn't know you were worried about me."

"Every second of every hour of every day and every night. If you knew how white-hot my anger at you was for disappearing on me without a trace... It took until that room, I think, to finally forgive you for your disappearing act."

"You forgave Nora a lot faster."

"I knew where she was. I knew she was safe. And she was gone one year, while I didn't see you for a decade. When I did see you again, you were dying in a hospital bed."

Silence again. A deep and honest silence.

"So," Søren said as he stretched out his long legs and crossed them at the ankles, crossed his arms over his chest and shrugged, "That's why I tend to gravitate toward Vivaldi's 'Winter' when I'm thinking of you. It worked once before, playing 'Winter,' and then there you were. Maybe it would work again. And so it has, finally."

Kingsley took a tenuous step forward.

"I have a secret for you. It's not my secret but I'll tell you anyway."

"I'm intrigued," Søren said and leaned back on the piano bench, arms crossed, ankles crossed.

"It's about your piano. Do you know how *la maîtresse* was able to afford to buy you a fifty-thousand dollar Bösendorfer piano?"

"I've always been afraid to ask."

"A wealthy man came to me with some *special* requests. Nothing she hadn't done before...except he was the son of a mafia don. You know how she despises the mafia. She turned the job down flat. Then she saw your piano for sale and called me back, said she'd do it. That was when you two were apart because you were being such a bastard about her working for me. And still, she still did that for you."

Søren glanced away, at the fire.

"No piano is worth that," Søren finally said.

"You are, though. To her. Now for my secret, one I even kept from myself. All these years, I resented you and hated her because I told myself that you loved her more than you loved me...but really, I think the truth is, she loved you more than I did, and I knew it, and that's what I resented."

Søren said nothing.

"If not *more*," Kingsley went on, "then *better.* She loved you better than I ever did. A brooding sexual obsession with someone you dated in high school doesn't really count as a relationship, does it?"

Søren smiled. "Not quite."

"I made passes at you. She made sacrifices for you. If this *was* a competition between me and her and you were the prize, she should win, hands down."

Søren said softly, "It's not a competition."

As if to prove that, he picked up the package tied in brown paper and gave it to Kingsley.

"This really was going to be your gift for this coming Christmas. If you open it, you won't be getting anything else this year. You've been warned."

"Empty threat," Kingsley said, though knowing Søren, he probably meant it. Still...he couldn't help himself. Søren slid slightly to the side and made room for Kingsley on the piano bench. Kingsley sat next to him and untied the twine.

He flipped the package over. When he pulled the paper apart, he knew what he was going to see: red and blue. A Paris Saint-Germain football shirt. Not the one Søren had originally gotten him all those years ago, but a replacement. And every time Kingsley wore it in New Orleans, he would think of Søren and miss him.

But he didn't see blue and red. He saw gray.

Gray and burgundy.

He unfolded the t-shirt and stared at the scarlet words screen-printed across the heather gray fabric.

LOYOLA UNIVERSITY
New Orleans

The cartoon head of a red wolf peered over top of the college's name, baring its teeth.

"What…" Kingsley's voice trailed off. He had to catch his breath.

"I am, as of one week ago, on the shortlist to replace Father Juan Domenico as a professor of pastoral studies at Loyola University. He's retiring at the end of the next school year."

Once again, Søren had stunned Kingsley into silence.

"Apparently I'm a 'shoe-in' for the position—a Jesuit priest with two PhDs and nearly twenty years of pastoral experience at my own church. I'll move to New Orleans next January or February. Just like you said…one last winter here."

Finally, Kingsley found his voice, and as usual, it was the voice of doubt. "And it's going to happen? You can just…make a phone call and leave?"

"They've been attempting to transfer me for years. I've done everything I could to stay here, but only because it was close to Eleanor. Close to you. I don't need this house or this church. I need you. I need her. I need my family. If my family is in New Orleans, that's where I need to be."

"What if you don't get the job?"

"I'll come anyway."

Kingsley felt like panicking. It didn't seem possible that this was real, and if it wasn't he would never survive the joke being played on him. His heart was pounding like a million horses racing across a thousand fields. He couldn't sit still. He rose from the piano bench and stalked back and forth in front of the fireplace.

"If I need to leave the Jesuits and join the Diocese of New Orleans as a parish priest, I will," Søren explained. "There are priest shortages everywhere. It won't be a problem."

"What about Nora?" He was almost dizzy with shock.

"She'll come, too."

"She will?"

"If she knows what's good for her."

How did Søren do that? How could he make a threat sound so sexy? Or sexy talk sound so threatening?

He was right, though. Nora would go. She'd said as much, that she would run off with Søren anywhere if he asked her.

"And don't worry about Juliette," Søren continued. "She called me weeks ago and asked if there was any chance we could join you all in New Orleans. She really does love you, you know. One of these days you're going to have to accept that I love you, too."

Kingsley had to sit down. He didn't even bother looking for a chair. He sat down on the rug in front of the fireplace, back to the fire, eyes on Søren.

He lowered his head and closed his eyes, breathed through his hands. The floor creaked and he felt Søren sit down by him on the rug. Then two strong hands drew him down across Søren's lap and fingers slid under his shirt to stroke his back.

They sat there by the crackling fire, suddenly boys again who would break every rule to be together, even if it were only at night and far away from the prying eyes of the rest of the world.

"That summer we were apart," Kingsley said, "all I wanted was to see you again. Then school started and one night...it happened. You took me out to the woods and it was the best night of my life. It feels like that night again."

Lips touched his temple. Then Søren spoke three words.

"You did well."

It was that night again.

Slowly, Kingsley lifted his head. He was still clutching the shirt. He smoothed out on the floor in front of him and folded it carefully and rolled it into the classic "ranger roll," which he'd learned to do back in his days in the Legion.

"I should get home to Jules," Kingsley said. No overnight visits for a long time. Juliette wasn't due quite yet but it was still possible she could go into labor at any moment.

"Of course," his lover said. "It isn't as if we're running out of time to be together."

Kingsley stood up and held the gray t-shirt against his chest, as if afraid to let it go. Søren stood, too, stood close.

"Another secret," Kingsley said. "I want you to kiss me."

"That's not a secret."

"It's—"

Before Kingsley could get another word out, Søren had fallen onto his mouth. Their lips met, their mouths opened, their tongues touched. Kingsley breathed deep. The logs on the fireplace crackled and delicious smoke wafted through the room. The taste of Søren—like snow melting on his tongue—and the scent of the fire, and the rough grip of strong, cool fingers on the back of Kingsley's neck, and the wind outside rushing over the windows...all of it came together and turned the kiss into a winter symphony, and all that was missing was the mistletoe above them, but it could wait. If not this Christmas, then the Christmas after, or after that.

Søren pulled back from the kiss. "I shouldn't have said, 'Don't do this to me again.' What I should have said was—"

He gripped Kingsley by the back of the neck, hard enough to leave bruises and bring tears to Kingsley's eyes. He tilted Kingsley's head back, forcing his chin up.

"What I should have said," Søren repeated, "was 'You will *not* leave me again.' Will you?"

"No," Kingsley breathed, growing hard.

Søren smiled. "Good."

Then Kingsley was free. He caught his breath, met Søren's eyes, gave a small laugh. "That's all you had to say."

Søren returned to the piano bench and sat, long legs out and crossed at the ankle. Kingsley lightly kicked the bottom of his bare foot.

"You know, Nora will kill you when she finds out you're keeping this a secret from her," Kingsley said.

"Turnabout is fair play. She's keeping something from us, too, if you hadn't noticed."

Yes, he'd noticed.

"So you aren't trying to protect her?" Kingsley said. "You're just getting your revenge?"

Søren furrowed his brow. "You seem surprised by this."

"I love you."

"That," Søren said, "is also not a secret."

With a last smile, he turned back to his piano.

Kingsley asked, "Just out of curiosity, what other secrets are you keeping from me?"

Søren said nothing, only began to play the piano again.

Kingsley rolled his eyes and walked out into the winter night. Eventually he might learn a few more of Søren's secrets, but not all of them. A little mystery was always good for a romance.

On the way to his car, Kingsley caught himself smiling.

He was happy.

Very, very happy.

FIFTH MOVEMENT

MARCH CODA

CODA:

The concluding section of a dance.

CHAPTER SEVENTEEN

"WHAT'S THIS?" Nora asked as she was putting away their toys after a long, delicious session of pain play and sex. "Who gave you a Carnival mask?"

Søren had just come back into the bedroom after taking a shower. He was naked but for a white towel wrapped around his trim waist. No man lost in the Sahara had ever longed to lap up water as much as she wanted to lick the water droplets off Søren's strong, flat stomach.

"Souvenir from New Orleans. Kingsley bought it for me but decided it was too bizarre, even for him."

She looked at the mask a long time, then held it out to him. "Try it on."

He raised his eyebrow, but took the mask from her and put it on, tying it with black ribbons around the back of his head. "What do you think?"

Nora stared at the eerily faceless man

standing before her and was suddenly very cognizant that she was on her knees.

"I've had dreams like this."

❄

LATER THAT NIGHT, Kingsley's phone buzzed in his pocket. He took it out and saw he had a message from Søren.

Two words.

Thank you.

He replied, *For what?*

He wasn't surprised by Søren's response.

It's a secret.

FIN.

BONUS SHORT STORY

A BEAUTIFUL THING

While he was in Bethany, reclining at the table in the home of Simon the Leper, a woman came with an alabaster jar of very expensive perfume, made of pure nard. She broke the jar and poured the perfume on his head. Some of those present were saying indignantly to one another, "Why this waste of perfume? It could have been sold for more than a year's wages and the money given to the poor." And they rebuked her harshly.

"Leave her alone," said Jesus. "Why are you bothering her? She has done a beautiful thing to me."

MARK 14:3-6

Three months before The Siren...

❄

Nora drove to the music store at the other end of town and ignored her ringing phone the entire way. Maybe if she didn't answer it, Kingsley would forget about why he was calling her. December 12th meant Christmas was all of thirteen days away. She had shit to do that didn't involve beating up the mayor's younger brother.

She pulled into Theremin's as her phone bleated at her once more. With a growl, she pulled it out of her coat pocket.

"King, new rule. No kink at Christmas." She got out of her car and slammed the door behind her.

"Forty thousand dollars," was his answer.

Nora paused a moment to pick her jaw up off the sidewalk. "Okay, maybe kink at Christmas. What's the job?"

"One week in Las Vegas. All expenses paid."

Nora leaned back against her car hood and crossed her booted legs at the ankle. She held her coat tight around her neck. The temperature had dropped ten degrees since morning. By nightfall, it would snow. She could smell it on the air.

"Couple?" she asked.

"Only him."

"Fetishes?"

"Feet. Pain. Blood."

Nora sighed. She'd have to have her entire collection of needles professionally sterilized. Again. "Sounds pretty basic. What's the catch?"

For forty thousand dollars, there had to be a catch.

"No catch," he said. "Not really."

"King, don't bullshit a bullshitter. What's the catch?"

"His name is Victor Moretti."

"Motherfucker."

"Is that *oui* or *non*?" Kingsley asked, his throaty laugh sending the temperature back up ten degrees.

"It's hell no. Moretti? He's mob. You know I don't play with the mob."

"Victor is only one of the Moretti sons," Kingsley said. "He's never been convicted of any crime."

"You've never been convicted of any crime either. That's not saying much."

"He's not in the family business. If he was, he wouldn't have moved across the country to get away from it."

"To Vegas, where mobsters go to retire. King, he's the son of a fucking crime boss. Those people are the reason my dad was buried closed-casket, remember? You know my number one rule," Nora said as she headed toward the entrance of the Theremin's. "'Any job except the mob.' Tell him no, but be nice about it."

Nora hung up on Kingsley as she entered the store. She'd ordered a new guitar case for Wesley, and it had come in finally. She wanted to get it early since he'd be leaving her right after finals on the fifteenth to spend Christmas in Kentucky with his parents. So far, she didn't really have any plans for Christmas. Maybe she'd fly off to Jamaica for a week and spend it on the beach. Maybe she'd go to Paris and find a handsome stranger to seduce. She used to spend her Christmases at Kingsley's. After saying Christmas Morning Mass, Søren would have lunch with his sister Claire in Manhattan and then spend the rest of the day hiding out with her and Kingsley at the townhouse. They'd exchange presents and eat and drink too much. But then she'd left Søren, and Christmas hadn't been the same since then. She'd almost asked Wesley to stay with her, but knew that sweet boy would do it just so she wouldn't be alone. She couldn't ask him to miss Christmas with his parents. The crazy kid actually liked his family. What a concept.

Jews. That was the answer. She needed more Jewish people in her life. There. Now she had her New Year's resolution: Make more Jewish friends. Then she'd have people to party with while the rest of the world did the Christmas thing. Perfect plan. Jews, Muslims, Buddhists, and maybe some atheists. She'd get right on that.

The owner went into the back to get the guitar case. While Nora waited, she wandered. In a side room, she stopped short when she laid eyes on the most beautiful grand piano she'd ever seen. Solid black finish with gleaming golden guts on the inside.

Of course the inside of a piano wasn't called the guts, though. What was it called? Søren would know.

"Nice, isn't it?" The store owner had returned with the guitar case. "Imperial Bösendorfer. Fully refurbished. One owner. The wife of a Presbyterian minister."

"Presbyterian?" she repeated. "Damn Calvinists."

"Excuse me?" he said, clearly not understanding her.

"Never mind." Søren was the only man she knew who, when asked what his pet peeves were, would answer *Calvinism*. "It's amazing. How much is it?"

"It's actually very reasonable. It's on consignment and the family can't wait to get rid of it. Forty-five. Delivery and tuning included."

Nora's knees buckled at the figure. "Forty-five thousand?"

"I know," the owner said, shaking his head. "It's a steal. A new one would run you eighty."

"Little out of my price range, I'm afraid." She had enough money for the piano, but just barely. She also had a mortgage, a roommate to feed, and the dream of giving up work with Kingsley to write full-time. If she dropped forty-five thousand dollars on a piano, she and Wes would be eating ramen noodles for the next year. Either that or she'd better get a big fucking book deal real fucking fast.

"You should play it at least. A piano wants to be played."

Nora reached out and touched the keys without depressing them.

"No, I don't play. I have a..." She paused, searching for the right word. "A friend. He plays beautifully. Learned it from his mother and then mostly self-taught. One of those prodigy types."

"Professional?"

"Actually, he's a Jesuit priest. He plays with the symphony sometimes if they need him. He has a Steinway, but, well, it's kind of broken."

"Such a shame."

"Just the sustain pedal. Long story. Do you play?" Nora asked. She was dying to hear the sound of the Bösendorfer. Some of her happiest memories involved Søren and pianos.

"Not much anymore. But I have my own personal pianist I keep around here. Isaiah?" He called out the name, and a boy of about twelve came running from the other room.

"I'm here!" Isaiah announced, his voice so loud the keys of the piano vibrated.

"Isaiah takes lessons here," the owner explained. "His family's apartment's not big enough for a piano. I let him come practice here whenever he likes."

"Nice to meet you." Nora held out her hand and Isaiah only stared at it. "Don't be scared. I know strange white ladies are terrifying, but I won't bite you. Probably not, anyway."

The boy grinned broadly and held out his hand. She shook it with vigor.

"Good handshake," she said. "Strong hands make for a better pianist. Will you play something for me?"

"Yes, ma'am," he said with gusto as he threw himself down onto the piano bench. He cracked his neck and knuckles and wiggled his fingers over the keys. "Any requests?"

"Play a Christmas song," Nora suggested. "Any one you like."

"I like 'em all. But I just learned this one."

He inhaled and closed his eyes. When he opened them again, the blustery boy had transformed into a professional musician. He brought his fingers down onto the keys. The familiar haunting strains of "O Holy Night" filled the store.

The piece brought back a thousand memories. How she loved this song...how much it moved her every time she heard it...how she couldn't hear it without wanting to fall onto her knees and adore the God who had created men and music.

How old had she been? Twenty-four? Twenty-five? One night in early December, she'd gone to the rectory at midnight and found Søren at the piano playing this very piece...

❄

HE KNEW she was coming to him that night, and he knew the song was her favorite. As he played, she came to him and sat on the floor next to the piano bench, resting her head by his thigh. As the last notes rang out and died, he had laid a hand gently on the side of her head. Without a word he bade her to stand. He didn't need words to give her orders. She could read his face, his eyes, his body language like a book. He snapped his fingers, and she reached under her skirt to pull off her panties. Søren lowered the fallboard to cover the keys as she straddled his lap and leaned back against the piano. They kissed, tongues and lips mingling, for what felt like an hour. She ran her fingers through his blond hair. He slid his hands up and down her thighs.

"Please, Sir," she whispered against his neck.

"Please what?"

She growled in playful frustration. He hadn't hurt her yet. They'd done nothing but kiss. As long as he didn't hurt her, he could kiss her and tease her and taunt her and touch her forever without needing to fuck her. It wasn't until he inflicted pain on her that he grew aroused enough that he had to have her. But she...she had to have him, and right now.

"Please...I need you inside me, Sir."

"Keep begging. It's under consideration."

He kissed her earlobe, her neck. He opened her blouse and kissed the swell of her breasts. And so she begged him as instructed. *Please, Sir...please... I'll do anything, submit to anything, give you anything, accept anything... Use me, abuse me, bruise me,* she begged him in a poem of desperation.

When his teeth bit into the soft flesh of her

shoulder, she knew it would happen. She gasped in pain as his previously gentle fingers dug into her hips hard enough she flinched.

The flinch did it. Seconds later, the piano bench sat toppled on the floor. Nora—then still "Eleanor"—lay on her stomach on the floor halfway under the piano. She braced herself with slow deep breaths and wasn't shocked when Søren pulled her shirt off and pushed her skirt to her waist. He landed the first brutal blow on the back of her thighs. She didn't look at what instrument of torture Søren wielded on her. Cane or crop or switch from a tree, it didn't matter. They all hurt like fuck.

Good. The greater the pain now, the greater the pleasure after.

After a dozen or more brutal blows to the back of her body, Søren dropped a crop onto the floor. It hit the hardwood with a softer sort of thud instead of a rattle of rattan. She braced herself for more pain. He might flog her next or whip her. She closed her eyes and let go of herself and any fears. No reason to be afraid. Søren loved her. He'd hurt her, but he would never harm her. He took more pleasure from inflicting pain than she took from an orgasm. She gave up her body to him, gave it up like a gift. And like a present, wrapped and given, he tore her open.

Søren straddled her thighs and gripped the back of her neck. Scalding candle wax landed on the center of her spine. Another drop hit a few inches higher. With Søren on top of her and holding her down, she couldn't flinch. She reached out for something, anything to grasp, and wrapped her fingers around the sustain pedal. She focused on the metal in her hand, its coolness and smoothness. The burning wax coated her spine and sent pain shooting through her entire body. It ended, finally it ended, and Søren pushed her onto her back. Her inflamed skin slapped the hardwood and she cried out in agony.

The agony was short-lived as Søren kissed her again, kissed her mouth, her neck, and spent as much time kissing her breasts as he had brutalizing her back. The moans that came from her were borne of pleasure, the deepest pleasure, the sort of pleasure that came only after suffering pain. The pain threw the pleasure into such sharp relief that sex without pain seemed illogical to her. Why even bother with someone so muted? So dampened?

So boring.

When Søren pushed her thighs wide open and brought his head between her legs, she felt anything but bored. His fingers dug deep into her and ground against her most sensitive spots while his tongue and lips against her clitoris brought her to the edge of orgasm and left her hanging there with knots of need coiling in her stomach and her hand still gripping the sustain pedal to steady herself.

Søren rose up and covered her with his body. He entered her hard and fast, and she came after the first few thrusts. After her climax, she relaxed and simply let him have her. She loved the pressure of him inside her, filling her up, moving within her, and the ragged but controlled tenor of his breathing.

After he came inside her, he slowly pulled out and dragged her into his arms. She panted against his chest as he stroked her hair and kissed her forehead.

"Did you enjoy that?" he asked as she lay across his lap.

"So fucking much. Only..."

"What?"

She eyed the piano and saw the sustain pedal hanging at a somewhat off-angle. "I think I broke your piano."

❄

THE SONG ENDED, and the final notes of "O Holy Night" played by young Isaiah shivered up Nora's spine.

"Thank you," she said to the boy. "You're very talented. I hope you never quit playing."

He shrugged. "Don't know. I'm on the basketball team at school. My dad, he wants me to quit piano and only play basketball. He thinks my sister should take the piano lessons. She doesn't like it, though. Just me."

"Why does he think your sister should take piano lessons and not you?"

"Says music is for girls. Mom tells him he's crazy and that it's good for me to know music so I can play in church."

"Music's for girls?" She looked up at the store

owner and winked at him. "I'll have you know the strongest, smartest, toughest, and most intimidating man I know also plays piano. What do you think of that?"

"That true?"

"Very true. And when he plays piano every woman in the room falls in love with him. Girls love musicians."

"That's true," said the store owner. "My wife said she didn't even notice I existed until she heard me playing saxophone."

Isaiah seemed to think it over. "Maybe I'll keep playing," he said. "Maybe I'll keep playing basketball, too. You know, double my chances with the ladies, right?"

"I like the way you think, kid." Nora chucked him under the chin. He scrambled off the piano bench and headed back to the other room of the store. "It's an amazing piano," she told the owner. "I love the sound. Richer than a Steinway."

"It's got beautiful bass notes. Holds the sound better. There's no piano like the Bösendorfer. They call them the Rolls Royce of pianos. If you change your mind, let me know. Like I said, price includes delivery."

The store owner left her alone with the piano. Nora touched the top and felt the ghost of a thousand concertos lurking in the polished wood.

Nora fished her phone out of her pocket.

"To what do I owe the pleasure?" Kingsley asked when he answered.

"Call Moretti back. Tell him I'll do it."

Kingsley said nothing and Nora rolled her eyes. Typical dominant trick—stop speaking to force the other to fill the silence.

"I'm at a music store," she explained.

Silence.

"It's December."

Silence.

"Did you know they call Bösendorfer pianos the Rolls Royce of pianos?"

Silence.

"It's almost Christmas. And it's almost his birthday, King."

Silence. And then...

"I'll tell him fifty or nothing," Kingsley said. "And I know him. He'll pay fifty. You can keep my cut this time."

"I knew you still loved him."

"I could say the same to you," Kingsley said.

The past year had been a cold war between her and Søren, between Kingsley and Søren. She didn't know what had started the war, but she knew she wanted to finish it. Maybe this would help. Even if it didn't, she had to give Søren the piano. She didn't know why, except for the reason Kingsley had named: She still loved Søren.

"I'll front you the money. Buy him the piano," Kingsley said.

"*Joyeux Noël,* King," Nora whispered.

"Merry Christmas, Elle."

She hung up the phone and called out for the store owner. "You said you deliver?"

"We deliver," he said, stepping back into the room with a broad smile crossing his wizened face.

"Sacred Heart Catholic Church in Wakefield. It goes to the rectory, not the church. You'll have to drive up to it around the block. It's tucked back in a little wooded area. You should be writing all this down. And it'll need to be delivered on December 21st. Do it after six, otherwise he'll be at the church working."

"Quite a Christmas gift you're giving," he said as he wrote down the details.

"Well..." She kissed her fingertips and touched the top of the piano in a benediction. "It's really for Christmas *and* his birthday."

❄

THAT FRIDAY, Nora boarded a plane for Vegas. A limo picked her up at the airport and took her to a sprawling mansion in Summerlin outside the Vegas city limits. Some sort of servant attempted to take her toy bag from her, but she waved him away as she entered the home. A man of about forty with a dark tan, a face that had once been handsome, and desperate eyes met her in the sunroom.

"Mistress Nora." He took her hand and kissed it. "It's an honor to have you in my home."

"Fuck your honor. You can do better than that," she said without a smile. "Floor."

He dropped to his feet and kissed the toe of her dirty boot.

"You know, Vic," she said as she pulled a riding crop out of her toy bag, "I really hate you mob guys. Bunch of fucking rich bullies. You act like royalty and you're all just lowlife thugs in expensive suits." Victor didn't disagree with her. He was too busy worshipping her feet with his tongue. "I hate the mob so much that I'm probably going to do some shit to you this week that you're not going to like. It'll be immoral, indecent, and very likely illegal. And you won't even get to fuck me. Not once. And then you know what I'm going to do?"

"What, Mistress?" he asked, looking up at her from the floor with groveling eyes.

"I'm going to leave this shit-hole house of yours and forget you ever existed. Now take off your clothes."

❄

Nora made it back to New York on December 20th. She spent a sleepless night in her bed wondering if she'd done the right thing fucking around with a mob guy. Victor hadn't been that bad. He, like her, had been an unwitting accomplice to the mafia far more than a willing participant. Victor hadn't chosen to be born of a crime boss and claimed to hate his father's world.

"Yeah, you hate the sinner," she said as she carved a shallow dollar sign into his back with a razor blade, "but you love that sinner's money, don't you?"

"I couldn't give it away, could I?" he asked as if she'd suggested he should put the money into a rocket ship and aim it at the sun. "Who would do that?"

"I know a guy who did." Søren had inherited a vast fortune from his monster father and kept not a penny for himself. "I'd let you meet him, but you don't even deserve to tie his shoelaces. Fuck you, Rich Bitch, you don't even deserve to tie mine."

She showed him that night and all week how little he deserved any mercy, compassion, or kindness from her. By the end of the week, he was so in love with her he offered her another fifty grand to stay through Christmas. As she walked out his front door without even a backward glance, she'd told him to shove his dirty money up his ass.

Knowing what a freak he was, he probably did.

The morning after returning, Nora called Theremin's and made sure the piano delivery would take place. They promised it would, and she spent the rest of the day working on her new book. Without Wes around, the house echoed with silence. She played some Christmas music, but it didn't fill up the emptiness in the house. She put on her coat and went for a walk, but the emptiness went with her. It wasn't in the house at all. It was inside her.

At six that evening, she put her coat on,

grabbed her keys, and got into her car. She drove to Wakefield and found herself parking across the street from Sacred Heart. The memories pressed in so close she had to shove them away lest she trip over them.

The parking lot was empty, thank God. No one around to recognize her, ask her what she was doing hanging around.

She stepped onto the cobblestone path that led down a tree-lined walkway to the rectory. It had snowed the night before, and a thousand footprints marred the new-fallen powder. The piano movers had come this way as they'd rolled the piano toward the house. She wished she'd been here to see the look on Søren's face. She'd given the piano anonymously, although she knew he'd know the gift came from her. After all, it was she who'd broken the sustain pedal on his Steinway. She sort of owed him a new piano.

As Nora reached the end of the path, she paused and cocked her head to the side. Through the windows of the rectory, she heard music emanating. She stepped closer and listened harder. Yes, music. Piano music. Søren was already playing his new piano. At the front door, she pressed her ear to the wood. She knew this song. Of course she knew it. She could even hear the lyrics in her head as the notes drifted through the door.

A thrill of hope, the weary world
rejoices...
For yonder breaks, a new and glorious
morn...
Fall on your knees...

Nora wanted to fall on her knees right then and there. She wanted to fall on her knees at Søren's side and rest her head on the piano bench like she had so many years ago. He played the song because he knew it was her favorite. He played even though he didn't know she could hear him. He played it for the memory of that night and all the Christmases they'd celebrated together in secret, each one more holy than the last.

She raised her hand and let it hover two inches from the door. When she knocked, the music would cease. He'd come to the door, open it and let her in, and he would beat her brutally, the way she liked it, and make love to her all night long.

Tonight was Søren's birthday. If she crossed the threshold tonight, she knew she would give herself to him. And not only for one night, but forever. She would lose Wesley. She would lose the life she'd made for herself. She'd even lose her name. Infamous, notorious Mistress Nora would turn back into Eleanor again if she returned to Søren.

Maybe he would let her be herself. Maybe he would let her keep her name. Maybe they would find a new way to be together. And maybe magic elves would show up at her house and crown her Queen of the Christmas Fairies.

Nice dream, but Søren had already told her when and if she came back to him, his first order would be to give up her job with Kingsley. She could be with Søren or she could be Mistress Nora. She couldn't be both.

Nora took a step back without knocking. But before leaving, she reached out and drew a heart with her fingertip in the window.

"Merry Christmas, Sir," she whispered into the crisp night winter air. "Happy birthday, my love."

When she walked away from the rectory, she didn't take the path. Instead, she crossed the unmarred snowy ground, leaving her small and familiar footprints behind her. At least he would know she had been there.

Sometimes that's all one needed to get through a hard day—someone just being there.

Maybe one of these days she would finally tire of being Mistress Nora, and she would go back to him and fall on her knees at his feet again. Maybe someday she'd give up the new life she'd made for herself and be his once more.

But not tonight. She'd already given him his Christmas and birthday present this year. He wasn't getting anything else from her.

❄

NORA DROVE the forty minutes back to her house. She'd make it through Christmas even if she didn't celebrate Christmas at all. Once upon a time, Christmas had been a fearful time for the early Christians, which is why they'd hidden their celebration under the mantle of a pagan one. The earliest Christians didn't celebrate Christmas at all, she told herself. She would be like one of them this year. She would skip Christmas, and it would be fine.

When Nora pulled into her driveway, she noticed a light in her window. Hadn't she turned them off when she'd left?

She opened the front door and found a teenage boy sitting in the middle of the living room floor wrapping a present. He was wearing jeans and a red-and-green plaid flannel shirt over a white V-neck tee. With the Christmas lights on the tree so bright and shining, even his sandy hair was glowing red and green.

"Holy shit, Wes. What are you doing here?"

Wes smiled at her, and it felt like summer had snuck in the house while winter had its back turned. "I told Mom and Dad I had to work over break and could only come home for a few days. We did Christmas yesterday. I got back this afternoon."

"But..."

"I know your dad's long gone," he said a little sheepishly. "And you said you and your mom don't get along. You don't do Christmas with your friends like you used to... I just didn't want you to be alone."

"Well. Damn."

"Since I don't want to be a liar, you're gonna

have to put me to work," Wes said. "Does your office need cleaned again?"

"You swore you'd never clean my office again after last time."

"Oh yeah," he said, blushing slightly. "That was...traumatic."

"I swear the butt plugs in the bottom drawer aren't for me," she said. "Mine are in my bedroom. The ones in my office are for a client."

"That really doesn't make it better, Nor. And I don't even want to know why you store them next to your spare printer cartridges."

"It's the *bottom* drawer. Of course I store them there. Where do you store your butt plugs?"

"In my butt. Duh."

"Why didn't I think of that?"

Nora knelt on the floor in front of Wesley's mess of wrapping paper, ribbons, tape, and bows.

"So no office cleaning. What can I do for you?" Wes asked, taping the ribbon to the bottom of his box. The wrapped box looked legitimately awful and absolutely adorable. She would teach him how to wrap a present the right way this week.

"You came back from Christmas with your family early to spend it with me. You don't have to do anything else. Nothing. You didn't even have to do that."

"I like giving big Christmas gifts. I can't buy you a new car or a house or anything, not like you need another car or another house. But I can give you me for Christmas. If you want me. You know, my company."

"Right," Nora said. "Your company." She was already picturing their Christmas together. Ice skating. Christmas present shopping. Going to the Nativity play at St. Luke's down the street. He hadn't just given her his company for Christmas. Now that she wasn't going to be alone, he'd given her Christmas for Christmas.

"You have to give me something to do or I'm a liar," he said.

"Telling men what to do is my specialty, kid. Go and get your guitar," she said. "You can sing for your supper. I need some Christmas music."

He brought out his guitar and quickly tuned it. "Any requests?" he asked as he picked out a few stray notes.

"Anything you like."

"Anything?"

"Anything but 'O Holy Night.'"

"Why not?"

"Because it makes me sad."

Wes narrowed his eyes at her and then nodded. He had learned by now that "makes me sad" was code for "makes me think of Søren." That was the last thing either of them wanted tonight.

"No worries." Wes grinned at her and all the sadness went away. "I don't even know how to play that one. How about this?"

Wes leaned back against the couch and stretched out his legs. Nora put a pillow on his shins and laid her head there, curling up like a child. With the tree lights lit and evening draping itself over the house like a black silk sheet and Wes here with her, it finally felt like Christmas. Wes began to play "Silent Night."

Silent night. Holy night. All is calm. All is bright.

And it was beautiful.

THE END.

ACKNOWLEDGMENTS

My deepest thanks to Bethany Hensel, Karen Stivali, and Kristi Falteisek for their help editing *A Winter Symphony* (especially Bethany, who had to read it twice when we sent her the wrong version). I couldn't do it without you, ladies. Merry Christmas and Happy New Year!

ABOUT THE AUTHOR

Tiffany Reisz is the *USA Today* bestselling author of the Romance Writers of America RITA®-winning Original Sinners series from Harlequin's Mira Books.

Her erotic fantasy *The Red*—the first entry in the Godwicks series, self-published under the banner 8th Circle Press—was named an NPR Best Book of the Year and a Goodreads Best Romance of the Month.

Tiffany lives in Kentucky with her husband, author Andrew Shaffer, and two cats. The cats are not writers.

Subscribe to the Tiffany Reisz email newsletter and receive a free copy of Something Nice, *a standalone Original Sinners ebook novella:*

www.tiffanyreisz.com/mailing-list

Lightning Source UK Ltd.
Milton Keynes UK
UKHW010746021220
374498UK00004B/706

9 781949 769180